THE
GIANTS'
TEA PARTY

D0542115

THE
GIANTS'
TEA PARTY

VIVIAN FRENCH
illustrated by Marta Kissi

WALKER
BOOKS

First published 2021 by Walker Books Ltd
87 Vauxhall Walk, London SE11 5HJ

2 4 6 8 10 9 7 5 3 1

Text © 2021 Vivian French
Illustrations © 2021 Marta Długołecka

The right of Vivian French and Marta Długołecka
to be identified as author and illustrator respectively
of this work has been asserted by them in accordance
with the Copyright, Designs and Patents Act 1988

This book has been typeset in Berkeley Oldstyle Book

Printed and bound by CPI Group (UK) Ltd, Croydon CR0 4YY

British Library Cataloguing in Publication Data:
a catalogue record for this book is available
from the British Library

ISBN 978-1-4063-9258-6

www.walker.co.uk

For Charlie,
with lots and lots of love
from Gran xxx
V.F.

For James,
my favourite person
in the whole world
M.K.

Chapter One

In the kingdom of Little Slippington, things were not going well.

"Does four and seven make forty?" King Ferdinand sounded hopeful.

"Oh, Pa!" Prince Maximilian Olivier Adolphus de Frogholme, known to his friends as Max, put down his book. "It couldn't possibly be forty. It's eleven."

"That's a shame." King Ferdinand sighed. "I was so hoping it was forty. I need forty gold pieces rather urgently. In fact, I need forty gold pieces EXTREMELY urgently."

Queen Gloria looked up from her knitting. "Is there a problem, dear?"

"A problem?" The king drooped over his piles of coins. "Yes. I can't pay the butcher, or the baker, or—"

"The candlestick maker!" Max said brightly.

"Why in the world would I want to pay a candlestick maker?" A suspicious look came over the king's face. "Have you been buying candlesticks and not telling me, Maximilian?"

It was Max's turn to look astonished. "You know I can't buy anything, Pa! I haven't had pocket money for months. And if I *did* have any money, which I don't, I'd buy something sensible like a book. What would I do with candlesticks?"

"They're very useful for putting candles in," Queen Gloria said. "Speaking of which, we need more candles. Could you put in an order, Ferdinand?"

The king groaned loudly and put his head on the table. "Didn't you hear what I said, Gloria? I can't pay for anything: I don't have enough left to pay for a box of matches, let alone a box of candles. We need gold, I tell you!"

"Have you looked down the side of your throne, dear?" The queen went on knitting. "I found a penny under one of your cushions only last week."

Max giggled. "You could get at least three matches for that, Pa."

"WILL NOBODY LISTEN TO ME?" the king roared. "We need GOLD! The castle's falling down, the moat's clogged up with waterweed, we haven't any servants, we haven't got an army, we haven't even got a cook—"

Queen Gloria looked offended. "Are you complaining about my cooking, dear? I made you a delicious boiled egg for your breakfast."

"But I had a boiled egg for my tea yesterday!" The king's face was purple. "And for my lunch. And the day before – and the day before that!

It's been nothing but boiled eggs since Cook left. I'm beginning to *look* like a boiled egg."

The queen put down her knitting and shook her finger at the king. "Temper, temper. And you've reminded me: the hen house needs a new roof. The poor little chickens get wet every time it rains and it puts them off laying. There won't be any eggs if it isn't mended very soon."

Max, suspecting his father might explode, jumped up from his chair. "We need to make a plan. Where do other people get gold?"

"They go to their treasure chest." The queen looked delighted with her suggestion, but the king growled at her.

"Our treasure chest is empty, Gloria."

"Then we must fill it again." Queen Gloria gave him a beaming smile. "You must ask someone with lots and lots of gold if we can have some. Easy!"

There was a long pause while the king struggled with a very unkingly desire to throw something at the queen.

At last he said, "It isn't quite as easy as you make it sound, Gloria. We'd need to give them something in exchange and we haven't got anything left. No carriages, no horses, no jewels – nothing." He pointed at his head. "I must be the only king ever to wear a crown made of paper!"

"But we've got Maximilian." The queen patted her son's hand. "He could marry a pretty princess with plenty of lovely gold."

Max looked horrified. "Mother! That's SO old-fashioned. I want to marry someone because I love them – not because they're rich!"

His mother shook her head. "Couldn't you consider marrying to save the chickens? Your father does so love a boiled egg."

"Absolutely not!" Max folded his arms. "I'd rather fight a dragon. Or a monster. Or a giant."

Queen Gloria stared at him for a long moment; then, with a shriek of excitement, she clapped her hands, and her knitting fell on the floor. "Of course! The GIANTS! The giants of Golden Hollow!

I remember my nurse telling me about them! They have cups, plates and teapots, all made of gold. Even their toothbrushes are made of gold!"

She stopped, looking puzzled.

"How can you clean your teeth with a gold toothbrush?"

Max didn't answer. He was thinking.

"I've never heard of these giants. Have you, Pa?"

King Ferdinand frowned. "No. And I don't like the sound of them. But are you sure your nurse wasn't telling you fairy stories, Gloria?"

"I'm certain." The queen's eyes were shining. "I can't imagine why I didn't think of them before! When I was a little princess I used to dream of having gold bedroom slippers, and a gold hot water bottle. We must get in touch with them straightaway!"

She turned to Max with a beaming smile.

"You won't need to marry a princess after all, dear. You can go and find the giants instead."

"Gloria!" King Ferdinand's eyebrows rose. "Are you suggesting we actually send our precious son to LOOK for giants?"

"It'll be quite all right, dear," Queen Gloria said calmly. "My nurse said they never hurt anyone, and my nurse was ALWAYS right. Besides, we need gold very badly. You said so yourself."

"Hang on a minute, Mother." Max took off his

spectacles, gave them a quick wipe with his thumb, and put them on again. "I've read about giants in my storybooks – some of them are very fierce. We need to find out the best way to talk to them."

The queen nodded. "How clever you are, Maximilian. You take after your dear father. So … will you look it up in a book?"

"I don't have the right kind of book," Max told her. "But I've heard of someone who might be able to help – the cook told me about her ages ago. She's called the Wisest One, and she told the cook exactly how to make a perfect rhubarb crumble. Why don't I go and see her, and ask her what we should do?"

Queen Gloria turned pale. "No, no, no! I won't allow it! I've heard about her too, and everyone says she's clever. *Very* clever. I've heard that she can addle people's brains with her cleverness!"

"That's why we've never been to see her before," King Ferdinand agreed. "She has *ideas* – and ideas are dangerous."

Max tried hard not to roll his eyes and sigh. "But isn't an idea exactly what we need just now, Pa? An idea to help us persuade the giants to let us have some gold?"

"Oh." The king stroked his beard. "I suppose so."

"So, can I go to see the Wisest One?" Max asked.

There was a long pause. Max held his breath … then had to let it out again. It was at least three breaths later when his father finally spoke.

"You can go as long as you're careful," he said, and Queen Gloria nodded her agreement.

"Be very, VERY careful. And be sure to wear your crown. It'll keep your brains from getting addled."

Chapter Two

Max had hoped to set out early the next morning, but his father kept him back.

"I was awake all night," the king said, "because I was thinking – you ought to have a horse. You're a prince, and princes ride on horseback."

Max looked at him in surprise. "But the stables have been empty for months, Pa."

"I know," the king said crossly. "I'm not silly, Maximilian. But we let the greengrocer keep his donkey in the little stable at the end, the damp one near the moat, and I'm sure you could borrow it. After all, he's never paid us any rent."

"That's because we owe him so much money," Max pointed out. "And it's a very grumpy donkey. It growls at me every time I go past it."

"Nonsense. Donkeys don't growl. Eat your breakfast while I go and talk to its owner." And the king stomped away, leaving Max staring gloomily at his egg.

The meeting with the greengrocer did not go well.

"Donkey's not for hire," the greengrocer said flatly. "My cart needs pulling. Goes slow enough as it is: doesn't need wearing out with *gallivanting*." The donkey looked as if it agreed with this statement, and the greengrocer went on: "And I'd like to point out that you still haven't paid your bills. Majesty or no majesty, bills need paying!"

King Ferdinand nodded enthusiastically. "Oh, indeed they do! And that's why we need your donkey, you see. My boy, Prince Maximilian, is going to find a fortune in gold, but a prince shouldn't walk. He ought to ride to seek his fortune—"

"Hang on a minute." The greengrocer's eyes had a greedy gleam. "Gold, you say? Hmm. Well. That does put a different view on the situation."

He put a proprietorial hand on the donkey's back.

"Let's see. What about me letting you borrow this highly valuable and hard-working animal in exchange for ten gold pieces?"

"What?" The king stared and the donkey opened its eyes wide.

"Ten gold pieces. Oh, and I want the use of a different stable. This one's too near the moat, which, if you haven't noticed, is full of waterweed that smells of old socks. It gives me pimples every time I go near it and it makes the donkey cough."

The king hesitated, and the greengrocer folded his arms. "Those are the terms. Take it or leave it."

The king took it. He returned to the breakfast room looking ruffled.

"That greengrocer is a difficult man," he announced. "And he's greedy. I had to promise him ten gold pieces for the use of his donkey – TEN!"

Max was horrified. "But what if the giants don't give me any gold?"

"It's important to think positive," the king said firmly. "Now, go say goodbye to your mother. She's got something special for you!"

Suspecting the worst, Max made his way to his mother's room. She was sitting up in bed

and looking pleased with herself. Beside her was a heap of dazzlingly bright and stripy material.

"Here you are, dear," the queen said, and she held it out to him.

"What is it?" Max asked.

"It's a cloak. You'll need a royal cloak." Queen Gloria pointed, and Max saw that one curtain was missing. "I took the curtain down and I stitched it myself. Do you like it?"

Max didn't like it at all, but he was fond of his mother and didn't want to hurt her feelings.

"It was very kind of you to think of it, Mother," he said, "and very, *very* wonderful of you to make it for me … but I think it might get a little bit in the way when I'm riding the donkey."

"It'll be fine." His mother lay back on her pillows with a smile. "Just swirl it round your shoulders. Now off you go, and be sure to bring back lots and lots of gold." She glanced up at the window. "I'm going to have a lovely time choosing new curtains…"

As Max walked slowly away, he was feeling anxious. He had never been an adventurous type of boy; he liked reading books, and staring at clouds, and daydreaming.

He was interested to meet the Wisest One because the cook had said her house was full of books, but he was far less certain about the giants. It seemed more than reasonable that they'd want to keep their gold for themselves, and that his journey to Golden Hollow would be a waste of time.

"Oh well," he told himself, "I suppose I'd better see what the Wisest One has to say… At least I can have a look at her books while I'm there. I'll say goodbye to Pa, then I'll go and find the donkey – and it *does* growl. It really does. I just hope it doesn't bite."

The donkey was not pleased to see Max. When he reached the stable door it turned its back on him and, when he opened the door and came in, it growled loudly.

"There," Max said out loud, "I knew it: it growls!"

"And *you've* got no manners." The voice was rusty, as if it wasn't often used. "No manners at all. Call yourself a prince? Huh! In my young days it was considered polite to introduce yourself, but now? Oh, no."

Max stared round, but there was no one else in the stable. "Did you… Did you speak?"

"Really!" The donkey snorted. "And I was given to understand that you like books. Did you never read about talking animals?"

"Well … yes." Max's eyes were very wide. "But I thought that was only in stories! I never thought talking animals really existed."

The donkey gave a weary sigh. "And where, you ignorant boy, do you think the people who wrote those stories got the idea of animals who could talk? From us, of course. Animals like me."

"But you never spoke to me before," Max said. He took off his spectacles and rubbed at them while he thought. "Why didn't you? You just growled!"

"Which only goes to prove how stupid you are," the donkey said sourly. "I thought everyone knew that donkeys don't growl. There I was, doing my best to let you know that I was a truly remarkable example of the equine race, but did you understand? Did you say, 'Goodness me! A growling donkey! How very unusual … I wonder if he can talk?' Oh, no. Not you."

"I'm very sorry," Max said. "Erm … do you talk to the greengrocer? He didn't mention it to Pa."

The donkey gave Max such a disapproving glare that the boy took a step backwards.

"Have you NO common sense?" he asked. "No respectable talking animal EVER speaks to an adult. They either decide they're imagining things and rush off to see a brain doctor, or they make immediate plans to display us in freak shows. Neither is at all satisfactory, so we keep quiet."

"I see." Max put his spectacles back on, stood up straight, and bowed. "How do you do? I'm Prince Maximilian, and I'm delighted to make your acquaintance. Might I know your name?"

The donkey snorted. "Ooh ... polite as pie now, are we? Too late. Manners is as manners does. And the name's Horace – so we'll have no more of the 'it does this and it does that', if you please."

"Of course." Max bowed again. "A pleasure to meet you, Mr Horace. And ... would it be all right if we got going?"

"Thought you'd never ask." Horace tossed his head. "You'll find my bridle hanging on the back of the door. And I don't do trotting, cantering or galloping. We'll travel at a nice steady walk, and that's that. By the way – where are we off to?"

"First, we're going to see The Wisest One," Max said, "and then we'll be going to Golden Hollow. Well, we *might* be."

"Golden Hollow?" Horace gave him a thoughtful look. "That's a fair old way … but I suppose it'll make a change from delivering carrots. Snip snap, lad! Hurry up with that bridle!"

Chapter Three

Unfortunately for Max, his mother and father both appeared at the front door of the palace to wave him goodbye, so his plan to quietly forget his cloak was a failure. He was obliged to ride away on Horace with the brightly striped curtain swirling round his shoulders. His mother blew him kisses, and his father gave him an approving nod as he and the donkey crossed the bridge over the weed-infested moat, and set out on their adventure.

As soon as they were out of sight of the palace Horace gave a loud grunt of disapproval.

"Whatever's that you're wearing?" he asked. "Makes my eyes hurt."

"My mother gave it to me," Max told him. "She likes bright things. It used to be one of her bedroom curtains."

"Can't imagine how she sleeps at night," Horace said. "But that's royalty for you. All show and no thought for others. They'll see you coming from the other side of the Hungry Marshes, and that's for sure."

Max shivered. "The Hungry Marshes? What are they?"

The donkey stopped dead, and turned his head to look at Max. "Are you serious? You don't know?"

"I've never done much geography," Max said apologetically. "When Pa and Mother started running out of money they had to get rid of my tutor. The prime minister was supposed to give me lessons, but all he knew about was other prime ministers so he didn't teach me much. Then he got fed up because he never got paid. After that I had lessons from the cook – I liked that much better because she taught me how to make a really good chocolate cake … but then there was no money at all and she went too. Now there's nobody."

"Hmph." Horace blew down his nose. "So you never thought to read a book about the kingdom? This land all around us, where you'll be king one day?" He blew down his nose a second time. "Although I suspect you'll never get to be a king, young man, as you're more than likely to get hopelessly lost somewhere for ever and ever and never be seen again."

Max shook his head. "I might have read something useful if Pa hadn't sold all our books. I hid a few, but none of them said anything about any 'Hungry Marshes'."

"Then you're extremely fortunate to have me as your companion," Horace replied. He started

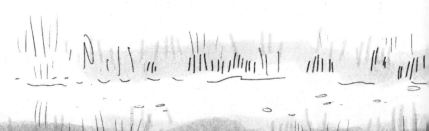

walking again and Max breathed a sigh of relief.
He had been secretly wondering if it would be rude
to shake the reins to hurry Horace along. Max had
ridden a horse a long time ago, but he was sure the
rules must be different when you were riding an
animal that could talk.

"So," Horace went on, "it seems you have a lot to learn. I, on the other hand, know a great deal. You get to hear all kinds of news and gossip when you travel around the kingdom delivering carrots and peas and potatoes. For instance, did you know that the Wisest One is extremely partial to sprouts?"

"Ugh." Max made a face. "I hate sprouts. But she likes books, doesn't she?"

Horace didn't answer, and Max saw that a horse and cart was coming towards them. The driver began to laugh when he saw the boy in an eye-wateringly bright cloak riding on a donkey, but he hastily changed his chuckles into a cough as he recognized the prince. Waving his whip in salute he trundled past, leaving Max red with embarrassment.

The cart was followed by various other horse-drawn vehicles and Horace was silent until at last he turned into a narrow lane that rapidly became nothing more than a track. Rough grass grew on either side and Max wondered how long it was since anybody else had come this way. He didn't want to ask Horace if he knew where he was going; he was sure that if he did, he would be given another lecture.

It was Horace who spoke first. "Not far now. And for goodness sake do try and be polite. I wouldn't call the Wisest One a witch, exactly, but you certainly don't want to upset her."

This was not comforting news. Max began to feel sick and to wonder if he should ask Horace to turn round and take him home. Only the thought of how disappointed his parents would be kept him from suggesting a tactical retreat … that thought, and the certainty that Horace would despise him.

"Does she have a real name?" he asked. "Is it all right to call her the Wisest One?"

The donkey sniggered. "She's called Agnes Bilberry, but you'd best call her 'Ma'am'. Nobody's called her Agnes for about a hundred years. She's probably forgotten her name herself. And look! Here we are."

Max looked up, and saw a strange ramshackle house with at least seven chimneys ahead of him. The windows were small and dark, and as he inspected them he was almost sure that one of them winked at him. A moment later it winked again, and Max's feeling of unease increased.

As Horace drew nearer, a door flew open and one of the chimneys sent up a twist of white smoke that curled into words… *Are you in possession of limpets, barnacles, slugs or snails? If not, you may enter.*

Taking a deep breath, Max slid off Horace's back. "Here I go," he said. "Wish me luck!"

"Certainly not." The donkey was emphatic. "Luck is a tricksy commodity at the best of times. Now hurry up! She's waiting for you." And he blew away a fly, then began to graze.

Chapter Four

Far, far away in Golden Hollow, an argument was taking place. Glom, King of the Giants, was shouting at his granddaughter, Hamfreda – and Hamfreda was shouting back.

"Gramps, you've got to do something … you've got to do something NOW! There's absolutely nothing to eat, there's no money left in the piggy bank, and the royal geese are starving – it's over a week since they've been fed. We've GOT to find some Papparelli roots!"

"Don't talk to me like that!" Glom stamped his foot and the walls shook. "I'm much too busy to

worry about the geese!
Throw them some crusts
and leave me alone."

Hamfreda clutched at her
head in exasperation. "But
GRAMPS! Why won't you listen
to me? There isn't any bread, and
anyway – it's not bread they eat.
Bread gives them stomach-
ache; they only eat those
special roots. And if the geese
aren't fed, they won't lay,
and if they won't lay,
there won't be any
more golden eggs,
and if there aren't
any eggs, we can't
pay the bills!

It's serious, Gramps, it really is. The tank where we grow Papparelli roots dried up because it leaked … and WHY did it leak? Because we couldn't pay the plumber!"

Glom glared at her. "Hamfreda, I'm only hours away from my very first flight! My flying machine just needs one or two final touches, and then I'll be up, up, up in the air. I'll fly high in the sky and find out what lies beyond the Hungry Marshes… Who knows what that might be? Lands full of wonders!" The king's eyes shone as he imagined it. "I'll be King Glom: world explorer. The first king of the giants to leave Golden Hollow. Books will be written about me, statues will be built, and my name shall go down in history."

Hamfreda groaned. "Oh, Gramps, when will you ever learn? How many flying machines have you built? Seven, is it – or eight? And none of them ever got off the ground."

Her grandfather scowled at her. "The Glommet Four flew for nearly three seconds."

"Only because you pushed it off a cliff," Hamfreda said. "And it broke into a million billion pieces, and you were covered in dreadful bruises."

"That is not the helpful attitude I would hope for from my only granddaughter. I'm hurt. Very hurt." Glom gave Hamfreda a reproachful look.

"I'm going back to my workshop to complete my masterpiece, the Glommet Nine. Do what you want about the geese. I have far more important things to consider – it's just occurred to me that I might need reinforcements on the wing struts…" And the King of the Giants stomped away.

Left on her own, Hamfreda gathered up the empty plates. Breakfast had been late, and nothing more than withered apples and overripe plums from the orchards. All the palace cupboards were empty and it was an age since either Hamfreda or her grandfather had eaten a proper meal. Glom hadn't noticed, but Hamfreda's stomach constantly rumbled in hunger.

As she took the plates into the kitchen, she glanced through the window and saw the royal geese standing patiently in the yard outside.

Waiting for their roots, poor things, she thought, and sighed as she looked at their hungry eyes. *If they were like ordinary geese, they could wander round the orchard and eat grass and berries … but, then again, if they were ordinary geese, they wouldn't lay golden eggs. I've got to find some way of feeding them.*

She dumped the plates in the sink with a crash and looked round to see if the bent and battered pots and pans hanging on the wall could give her any inspiration. A long time ago they had all been coated in gold, but it had gradually worn away and there was no way the coating could be replaced.

Over the years the flock of royal geese had steadily decreased in number, and the golden eggs they laid had to be put to more practical uses, like paying the few remaining servants and the endless bills that trickled through the royal letterbox. Hamfreda sighed again as she thought about the long gone glories of the past: her grandmother had once told her a story about owning a golden toothbrush… Hamfreda hadn't entirely believed her, but King Glom had promised it was true.

Now, as she stared at the enormous frying pan, Hamfreda wondered if she could still see the tiniest glint by the handle. Stepping closer she saw she was right, and she took this as a hopeful sign.

"All I have to do," she told herself, "is find enough food for the geese so they start laying again. But where will I find Papparelli roots? The only ones I've ever seen, we grew in tanks – I've no idea where they came from before that. I'll have to ask Gramps if I can look it up in his *Book of Really Useful Things*, and that means finding it in his workshop. Oh well: here goes…"

And, taking a deep breath of resolution, Hamfreda marched out of the kitchen and down the echoing corridor to her grandfather's workshop. The sign on the door said: *No entry! Not ever! Never, in fact! And that means YOU, Hamfreda!*

Hamfreda shook her head, knocked and went in.

Chapter Five

As Max walked into the Wisest One's house, another door opened in front of him. He hesitated and a crackly old voice called, "Don't dilly dally! Come! Come!"

Max did as he was told, but as he came through the doorway he stopped to stare. There were books in rows on crooked shelves that reached from floor to ceiling, books piled high in tottering heaps on the floor and books scattered all over the table.

The very old lady who sat beside the table was dressed in a strange black garment that seemed to be mostly pockets, and Max saw that each pocket held a book. The old lady herself was so wrinkled and whiskery and warty that she looked more like a lichen-covered rock than a woman, but her eyes were very bright as she watched Max staring round. At her feet was a large furry rug: only when it opened a yellow eye and winked at Max did he realize it was alive.

"Oh," he said. "*Oh* … OH! What a wonderful, WONDERFUL room!" And then, remembering his manners, he bowed. "I'm so sorry. I should introduce myself. I'm Prince Maximilian, son of—"

"King Ferdinand and Queen Gloria," the Wisest One interrupted him. "A foolish couple. What do you want?"

"Um…" Max was taken aback by this direct approach. "Well, I wondered if you could help me to find the giants of Golden Hollow?"

The Wisest One sighed. "So you're after their gold."

Max heard the disappointment in her voice, and blushed. "It's not for me—"

"I don't believe you." The Wisest One pulled a book from one of her pockets, sighed again, and began to read.

Max, at a loss, stood first on one leg and then the other while he wondered what he should do or say. His eye fell on the page she was reading and he gave a small squeak of excitement.

"I've read that book! I couldn't wait to know what was going to happen at the end… I stayed up all night to find out. Don't you just love the one-legged pirate who pretended to be a ghost?"

"Indeed I do." There was warmth in the Wisest One's answer and she put the book down. "So, you like reading?"

Max nodded. "I like it better than anything!" He gestured at the walls of books. "Have you read them all?"

"All." The Wisest One patted the book beside her. "And some several times over."

"I read that book three times." Max's eyes shone. "I'd have read it again and again if Pa hadn't sold it…" His voice faded away. Was he being disloyal to his father? "I'm sure he wouldn't have got rid of all my books if he hadn't run out of money."

"Huh! Is that so?" The Wisest One raised her bristling eyebrows. "Now … about these giants. Do you realize you'll have to cross the Hungry Marshes to reach them?"

"Horace mentioned them," Max said. "Are they – are they very scary?"

The animal lying at the Wisest One's feet sat up and Max took a startled step back. It was considerably larger than a cat, but it didn't look like a leopard, or a tiger or, indeed, anything he had ever seen in his animal books. It did have spots, but then again it also had stripes and blotches and tufts on the end of its tail. What *was* it?

"I've heard they're absolutely TERRIFYING, sweetie!" the animal said. "Those marshes gobble up everyone who tries to cross them. And after they've gobbled them up, they burp a few times and wait for more…"

"Be quiet, Caromel," the Wisest One said. "You've never been to the marshes: you're just trying to scare the boy." She turned to Max. "There is a way you could cross the Hungry Marshes, if you're prepared to take the risk. I've read about it. They'll let you cross … if you keep them fed."

Max felt his legs wobble. "What do they eat?"

The Wisest One picked up the book that she and Max had both enjoyed. "Stories. That's what they like."

"So what do I do?" Max asked. "Do I have to give them books?"

The Wisest One snorted with laughter. "Oodly doodly! Do you think a marsh can read? No, you have to *tell* them stories. And don't stop."

"Not even for a second," Caromel said brightly. "If you stop, sweetie, I expect you'll sink. Up to your knees, up to your waist, up to your neck … and then? Glug, glug, glug. And BURP!"

Trying hard not to look agitated, Max asked, "And what about the giants?"

"Never met them. That'll be up to you." The Wisest One bent down, picked up a book from the floor and held it out. "Here. This might help you. Now, I'm bored with talking, so you can go. I want to finish my story." She gave the prince a dismissive nod, then paused. "Come and see me when you get back. IF you get back, of course." Then she opened her book and was immediately engrossed.

Max opened his mouth to thank her, but it was so obvious she wouldn't notice that he said nothing. Tucking his present under his arm, he made his way out of the house and found Horace lying under a tree. Sitting down beside the donkey he opened the book expecting to find a map, or a description of the Hungry Marshes or, even better, advice on the best way to speak to giants.

The pages were blank.

Max fluttered the pages, hunting for at least one page of writing … but there was nothing. He turned it upside down, but it made no difference. There was still nothing.

Horace opened one eye. "Oh. You're back." He yawned, and heaved himself to his feet. "So … what's the plan?"

"Just a minute." Max's thoughts were whirling round and round. He wasn't sure why he didn't immediately say that he was going home, because it was all much too difficult. Surely that would be the sensible thing to do? He looked once more at the book. "The Wisest One must have given it to me for a reason. And she didn't say not to go…"

Horace flicked his ears impatiently. "Hurry up and decide. You'll wear your brain out with all that thinking."

Max took a deep breath. "We're going to find the giants." He put his glasses back on. "Which way are the Marshes?"

Chapter Six

It was almost impossible to find King Glom in his workshop. The floor was inches deep in sawdust, hundreds of planks of wood were stacked in wobbling piles, ropes and pulleys hung from the ceiling, and huge dirty canvas sheets were heaped in every corner. Hammers and saws and nails were dumped in random pots and boxes, and chewed ends of pencils and broken rulers littered every surface. Cobwebs floated in the dusty air and Hamfreda brushed them aside as she cautiously made her way towards the sound of muttering and thumping.

"GRAMPS!" she said loudly and Glom looked up with a start. Hamfreda had expected him to be furiously angry at being interrupted, so she was astonished to see that he was beaming at her.

"I've found the answer!" he announced. "Well done, Hamfreda – I got to thinking about your geese and I was inspired. Totally inspired!"

He seized Hamfreda's hands and twirled her round and round.

"I've abandoned the Glommet Nine. Waste of time, it'd never work. I'm going to build the Glommet Ten, instead! I was thinking about what you said, and I thought: geese fly, don't they? And how do they fly? They flap their wings *and* they make a honking noise. THAT'S where I've been going wrong … my flying machines don't make a noise and the wings don't flap! But I need to study a goose or two to see how they work. Could you fetch me one? And a trumpet? I'll definitely need a trumpet. Trumpets honk, you know."

"Not just now, Gramps." Hamfreda shook her head. "I've got to find some Papparelli roots. Can I look at your *Book of Really Useful Things*?"

The king looked vague. "Do I have a book like that?"

"Yes," Hamfreda said, "you do. I want to find out where Papparelli roots grow so I can pick some." A thought came to her and she gave her grandfather a cunning look. "If I can find the roots, I can feed our geese – then they'll lay lots of golden eggs, and I promise I'll buy you the very loudest trumpet ever!"

Glom's smile faded a little, then broke out again. "Let's find that book!" And he dived into a chaotic pile of crumpled paper, torn envelopes, books and general rubbish.

"Aha!" With a cry of triumph he unearthed a battered brown book and waved it in the air. Hamfreda looked at it and shook her head.

"No, Gramps. This is *Fifty Ways to Peel a Parsnip*."

"Oh." Her grandfather dived back into the pile. Five minutes later he had found *How to Learn to*

Dance the Rumplepooza, The Jokes Of a Humorous Hedgehog and *Snail Taming for Beginners* … but no *Book of Really Useful Things*.

"Let me look," Hamfreda said, but all she found was a deserted mouse's nest in what looked like an old-fashioned cookery book, and a half-eaten chocolate biscuit.

Her grandfather pounced on the biscuit; Hamfreda sank back on her heels and sighed.

"Maybe it's not here after all," she said sadly. But even as she spoke, her eye was caught by the cover of the book the mouse had chosen for its nest, and she looked more closely. "That's it! This is the *Book of Really Useful Things*!"

Her heart beat faster as she picked the book up and inspected it. Most of the pages were chewed and many were missing, but it was possible to read a little here and there. Hamfreda flicked through *M*, *N* and *O* … and gasped.

"Papparelli roots! It's here!" She eagerly read what was left of the page. "'Damp, marshy conditions… Unable to be grown in Golden Hollow due to the dry sandy soil… Many plantations can be found in or near—'"

The entry came to an abrupt mouse-eaten stop. There was only a large hole where the vital words had been written, and the next thing Hamfreda could read were articles about *Quacking*, *Quadrupeds* and *Quests*.

"Oh, BOTHER!" she said.

"What's that?" Glom looked over her shoulder.

"It's been eaten by a stupid mouse." Hamfreda flung the book down. "It says 'damp, marshy conditions' but it doesn't say where."

"Oh dear." Glom pulled at his hair until it stood up on end. "The Hungry Marshes," he said at last. "No other marshes round here that I know of. It has to be the Hungry Marshes!"

"But they're miles and miles and MILES away," Hamfreda said gloomily. "How will I get there?"

King Glom folded his arms and looked extremely pleased with himself. "Easy! We'll go in Glommet Six."

"But it doesn't WORK, Gramps!" Hamfreda rubbed her eyes and tried not to cry. "None of your beastly inventions do!"

Her grandfather looked offended, but he said, "It may not fly, Hamfreda, but it goes very fast along the ground. If we both pedal, we'll be there in no time."

"What?" Hamfreda stared at Glom. "WE? You mean … go together? Both of us?"

"That's right." The king nodded. "Get your coat on, and I'll get Glommet Six out of the shed – I'll see you in the palace yard." He rubbed his hands together. "I'm going to get the very loudest trumpet ever! I can't wait." He stomped off to get ready, while Hamfreda skipped across the yard to get ready.

The seven royal geese watched her with beady eyes. This was the girl who fed them; they needed to keep close to her. They were hungry. Wherever she was going, they were going to go too.

The Glommet Six was not an attractive machine. It had several more wheels than it needed, four mysterious levers, three propellers, a wobbly flagpole and a gloomy looking fish by way of a figurehead, but Glom was right.

When he and Hamfreda pedalled together it *did* go fast … faster than they could have walked, at any rate. The few giants they passed bowed and saluted without much curiosity. The king's

aeronautical aspirations were well known, and they shrugged as they went on their way.

"That'll be another crash," they told each other. "Best to pretend we're busy. Don't want to have to pick up the pieces."

The royal geese, who were much too thin and feeble to fly, had insisted on flapping and fluttering onto the back seat. Now they were squawking loudly as they tried to keep their balance.

Hamfreda had done her best to shoo them back home, but they looked so determined she gave up. *After all*, she thought, *if I find the roots they can have their dinner straightaway. And if I don't...*

This was a thought she didn't finish. It was too depressing.

Chapter Seven

The road to the marshes lay through the villages of Grunge, Splice and Nether Dread. Max had never been to any of them and he looked around with interest as Horace walked steadily on. The villagers gave him a brief glance, then carried on with their everyday business of pickling walnuts and peeling onions.

It wasn't until they reached Nether Dread that a tall, thin man with drooping whiskers rode up beside them, accompanied by a small plump woman who was pushing a wheelbarrow full of brightly coloured little bags.

The tall man greeted Max with a cheery, "Hail, fellow traveller! And where might a handsome young lad like you be going?" His very white teeth shone in the sunshine as he smiled, giving him the look of a jovial crocodile.

"Aw! He's a bonny lad," the woman agreed. "Off to visit your auntie, are you?"

Horace had been silent since they first reached Grunge, and Max was pleased to have someone to talk to. "I'm going to Golden Hollow," he said. "Have you been? Have you met the—"

"HEEHAW, HEEHAW, HEEHAW!"

Horace exploded into such loud braying that Max was unable to finish his sentence. The tall, thin man put his head on one side and waited until Horace finally stopped, out of breath and wheezing hard.

"My word! What an energetic animal."

The man's teeth flashed in the sunlight as he smiled and smiled and smiled.

"And are you riding him all the way to your destination? Where was it, now? Oh yes. Golden Hollow."

He turned to his companion.

"Now, have a guess, Mrs Crimp! What do you think this fine young fellow is off to do?"

Mrs Crimp smiled too, and her teeth were unusually sharp and pointed. "I rather think he's off to find his fortune, Crimpie dear."

Mr Crimp threw back his head and laughed very loudly before turning back to Max. "Did you hear her, my friend? What a woman! So, is she right? Are you off to seek your fortune?"

"Yes!" Max nodded. He thought Mr and Mrs Crimp were delightful; their smiles were so wide and they were so very friendly. "I'm going to find the giants."

"Giants?" Mr and Mrs Crimp stared at him. "Did you say *giants*?"

"The giants of Golden Hollow," Max explained. "They have lots and lots of—"

"HEEHAW, HEEHAW, HEEHAW!" Horace brayed and Max looked at him in alarm.

"What's wrong, Horace?" he asked.

Horace gave him a baleful stare and said nothing. Max stroked his velvety grey ears in what he hoped was a soothing manner.

"I don't know what's got into him," he apologized. "He's not usually so noisy." Leaning towards Mr Crimp, he added, "He's VERY clever. He's going to show me the way."

Mrs Crimp gave a trill of laughter. "A clever donkey? And you're off to find giants? Whatever next! Parsnips growing on a pin, perhaps?"

Mr Crimp edged a little closer. "Your donkey knows the way, does he? What an interesting animal. I don't suppose you'd care to sell him?"

Max drew back. "Oh no! He belongs to the greengrocer. I couldn't possibly sell him. Besides, he's my…" He paused, not entirely sure how Horace would feel about being called his friend. Deciding to be careful, he went on, "He's my companion – and he's helping me to get rich."

Horace let out a long exasperated sigh, but Max didn't notice.

"The giants are supposed to have lots of gold, so I'm going to see if I can persuade them to help my poor mother and father. They've had nothing to eat but boiled eggs for more than three months."

As Max spoke, the enormity of the task ahead suddenly hit him and he shook his head gloomily.

"Although I don't see why the giants *should* help. I don't have anything to give them in exchange."

Mr Crimp's crocodile smile grew wider as his eyes narrowed. "What a very lucky thing we met." He lowered his voice. "Mrs Crimp and me, we're traders. We trade in something extraordinarily special and unique. Isn't that right, Mrs Crimp?"

"Oh yes, indeed." Mrs Crimp nodded so hard her many chins shook like jellies.

"Now you tell me, young man … what does everyone want? They want—" she looked to left and right, as if there might be listeners, then she whispered— "magic!"

"Magic?" Max's eyes opened wide. "REAL magic? Like in the storybooks?"

"Exactly!" It was Mr Crimp who answered. "Mrs Crimp, enlighten our dear friend!"

Mrs Crimp put down her wheelbarrow, held out her arms and recited:

> *When you're grumpy, when you're sad,*
> *Nothing's good and life is bad,*
> *When you're feeling bleak and blue*
> *We've got just the cure for you!*
> *Take our cure is what we say*
> *You'll be laughing every day!*

"Goodness," Max said. "It must be very special, this cure of yours."

"Oh it is." Mr Crimp nodded. His teeth were dazzling. "Very special indeed. As my dear Mrs Crimp told you – it's magic!"

Chapter Eight

"So," Mrs Crimp said, "now you know about our magic cure, perhaps you can see how we could help you?"

Max wasn't entirely sure that he understood, but he agreed politely. "That would be very kind."

Mr Crimp leant down from his pony and picked up a handful of the little bags in the wheelbarrow. With a flourish he presented them to Max.

"There! Take these to your giants, and sell them for glittering gold."

Mrs Crimp clasped her hands to her chest. "Save your poor parents, young man, and be a hero!"

"What are they?" Max looked curiously at the little bags. They were very light, and they rustled as he took them from Mr Crimp.

"These, young man, are magic bags." Mr Crimp's voice was hushed. "Put one under your pillow and, when you wake up, the world will be full of joy and happiness."

Mrs Crimp patted Max's arm. "The ache in your toes will be gone …"

Mr Crimp joined in: "... the spot on your nose will be gone ..."

"... you'll sleep like a baby at night ..."

"... and everything wrong will be right."

"That sounds wonderful," Max said. "What are they made of?"

Mr Crimp leant forward, and lowered his voice further to a conspiratorial whisper. "Inside each of these bags, young man, is a mixture of secret herbs."

Max's eyes widened. "Secret herbs?"

Mr Crimp nodded. "So secret that nobody knows their names. They were gathered on the stroke of midnight by the seven daughters of the harvest moon. As the daughters picked them they sang magical songs that were woven into the fabric of each bag ... but be warned!"

Mr Crimp came even closer and Max could feel the man's whiskers tickling his ear.

"You must never, EVER open the bags, or the magic will fail. Isn't that true, Mrs Crimp?"

"Oh yes, Crimpie darling. All the magic will float away … up into the midnight sky." Mrs Crimp was smiling so widely that Max couldn't help wondering if she was laughing at him.

I'm sure she's not, he thought. *She's just happy to help.* Out loud he said, "Thank you very much indeed, but are you sure you can spare them? If they're so very special, don't you want to keep them?"

"You're right, young man." Mr Crimp turned to Mrs Crimp. "He's a clever one, isn't he, Mrs Crimp?"

"As bright as a button!" Mrs Crimp agreed and her smile was dazzling. "The brightest, shiniest button in the box!"

Mr Crimp whipped a piece of paper and a pencil out of his pocket.

"We want you to have those magic bags, my dear young man. We really, really, REALLY want them to bring you a fortune."

He coughed, then gave Max a beguiling wink.

"But I'm sure you'll agree it's only fair that you bring us back a few pieces of gold by way of a

… what shall we say? By way of a token of your gratitude."

Max, taken aback by the suggestion but too polite to say so, nodded. "Of course."

"So sign this paper for us, my dear young man," Mrs Crimp said. "Just write your name." She patted Max's arm some more. "Of course we trust you – absolutely! But we traders need to be ever so careful. Forgive us, dear boy." She looked solemnly at Max. "Do say you understand."

"Oh, I do!" Max took the paper and pencil, and at once Horace began to shiver violently.

"Horace! I can't write properly if you shake like that," Max protested.

Horace went on shivering. Mrs Crimp's smile began to look fixed, but she said brightly, "Tell me your name, dear, and I'll write it for you."

"Maximilian," Max said. A curious look passed between the Crimps.

"Not … not Prince Maximilian?" Mr Crimp asked, and when Max agreed that he was, Mrs Crimp sank into a low curtsy.

"Well I never did," she said. "To think that Mr Crimp and I might be of use to a real live prince. Here, Your Highness."

She thrust another handful of bags in Max's direction.

"Take them and sell them to the giants for five pieces of gold a bag."

Mr Crimp held up a finger. "No, no, Mrs Crimp! We're talking to a member of the noble royal family.

Just fancy! Those giants will be most impressed. Our royal friend should ask for ten gold pieces per bag, at the very least. And we'll be quite content with – what shall we say? Fifty pieces of gold?"

Mrs Crimp put her head on one side and her teeth looked sharper than ever as she smiled. "I'm sure a handsome young prince will do well. Let us say … a hundred pieces of gold!"

Max was feeling increasingly anxious. It sounded like an enormous sum of money, and he wasn't at all sure that he would be any good at bargaining with anyone, let alone a giant.

Seeing the doubt in his eyes, Mrs Crimp snatched the piece of paper away from him, and hastily scribbled on it.

"There!" she said. "I've written your name for you. Just put a little cross here, dear, and then we'll be fine and—"

Her words were never answered. Horace had taken off like an arrow from a bow, leaving Mrs Crimp standing with her mouth open.

Mr Crimp stamped his feet and swore loudly for some considerable time. Then, gathering himself together, he said, "No worries, Mrs C. We'll catch him on the way back, sure as my name's Carniver Crimp."

Digging under the remaining bags in the wheelbarrow, he pulled out an ugly looking cudgel and whirled it round his head. "He'll have to come this way. Only road there is."

Mrs Crimp bared her teeth. "And he could have

had it so easy! If he'd signed that paper, we'd have had proper legal ownership of all his gold."

Mr Crimp gave a nasty chuckle. "We'll still have ownership, Mrs C. What's more, we'll have ownership of a nice little donkey as well. We'll buy a cart for him to pull and you can ride in style!"

Mrs Crimp had a sudden worrying thought. "But what if he doesn't find enough gold? I want to be rich, Crimpie – really truly properly rich, and that boy – well, he seemed the wishy washy sort to me. Suppose he takes one quick look at the giants, then runs home to his darling mummy and daddy?"

"Now there's a thing." Mr Crimp's face crumpled in thought. "Hang on a minute…" His face cleared. "Of course! We take him hostage! He's a prince, isn't he? So his darling mummy and daddy are the king and the queen, and kings and queens are sure to be rich." He sniffed. "All that nonsense about eating boiled eggs. Ha! Rubbish, I'd say. They'll have treasure chests full of rubies and diamonds and pearls."

Mrs Crimp nodded. "Keep talking, Crimpie."

"So—" Mr Crimp's teeth were dazzling. "We agree to return him safe and sound in exchange for a large reward, and we live happily ever after."

"And if he does bring back loads and loads of gold, we get to keep that too! Crimpie, darling, you're a genius!" Mrs Crimp flung her arms round her husband. Then, after a pause, she added, "But I think I'd rather have donkey-skin boots than ride in a cart."

Mr Crimp smiled his toothiest smile. "Your wish is my command, Mrs C. Now … let's sit and wait."

Chapter Nine

It took some time to leave Golden Hollow. There was a steep slope on every side, and both Hamfreda and Glom were puffing hard by the time they reached the top. As they stopped to stretch their legs and recover their breath, Glom pointed into the distance. "See that glimmer of water? That must be the marshes."

Hamfreda looked at him in surprise. "Don't you know?"

"Why would I?" Her grandfather shrugged. "Nobody's ever made any maps. We've never needed them. We've always been perfectly happy in the Hollow, us giants ... except for me."

Glom gave himself a congratulatory thump on the chest.

"I'm different."

He waved an enthusiastic arm and one of the propellers snapped off.

"You're the same, Hamfreda. It wasn't hard to convince you finding the marshes was a good idea."

He waved the other arm, and dislodged the flagpole.

"It comes of being a king, you see. That's how I got to be king. By having good ideas."

Hamfreda opened her mouth to say that, actually, going to the marshes had been HER idea, but decided against it. Glom was always at his best when he believed he was in charge.

"You're very clever, Gramps," she agreed. "Now, shall we get going again? The marshes don't look as far as I thought they would be."

"And it's downhill all the way," Glom said. A thoughtful look came into his eye. "Maybe we could try flying? Just a little bit?"

"No, Gramps." Hamfreda was firm. "Sorry, but I feel safer travelling on the ground."

And she climbed back into the Glommet Six; her grandfather, sighing heavily, followed her.

Prince Maximilian Olivier Adolphus de Frogholme would not have agreed that it was safer travelling on the ground. As Horace galloped along, Max bumped and jolted until his teeth rattled, and it was all he could do not to fall off. Hanging grimly onto the donkey's neck with one arm, he clutched the magic bags with the other and shut his eyes tightly as they flew along the path.

When, at long last, Horace slowed to a respectable walk, Max sat up, opened his eyes and looked about him. Straight ahead he could see a wide open space – and he could hear a low murmuring noise, as if hundreds of people were gathered together in a crowd.

"Where are we?" he asked, before adding reproachfully, "I thought you never went at a gallop. I nearly fell off!"

Horace snorted loudly. "Had to get you away from that couple of tricksters."

"Tricksters?" Max looked at him in surprise. "You mean Mr and Mrs Crimp?"

"Who else?" Horace snorted again. "Mr and Mrs Crocodile, more like. I've never seen so many teeth! All waiting to snap up a silly young fledgling like you."

"I'm not silly," Max protested, but at the back of his mind he was remembering Mrs Crimp's sly smile. He thought for a moment, then asked, "How were they tricking me?"

"Oh my hooves and haystacks!" The donkey groaned. "Don't tell me you believed all that moonshine about magic herbs?"

Max's jaw dropped. "You mean … do you mean they aren't magic? But they were picked at midnight! By … what was it? 'Daughters of the moon'?"

"Believe that," Horace said with a sneer, "and you'll believe anything. Have a look and see if I'm right."

"But I mustn't," Max protested. "That'll let the magic out…" He saw Horace's expression and stopped. With trembling fingers, he undid one of the bags and shook out the contents. There were scraps of torn-up white paper … and nothing else.

"Oh," he said as he looked. "OH."

"Told you so." Horace was smug. "Tricksters."

"Cheats and swindlers, sweetie. All teeth and no truth," added a voice.

Max swung round, but could see no one. It wasn't until Caromel dropped down from a tree that he realized who had spoken, and he looked at the big cat-like creature doubtfully. "Hello."

Caromel beamed at him. "Oh, my precious poppet – don't tell me you aren't delighted to see me! Not after I've come all this way to keep you company … I'd be too, too sad. I've never seen a giant, you see, and I've never seen the Hungry Marshes either." She put a large furry paw on Max's arm. "Don't forget you have to tell them stories, or you'll be gobbled right up! Glug, glug, glug! Oh, what fun!"

Horace, much to Max's surprise, wiggled his ears happily. "Good to see you again, Miss Caromel."

"Thank you kindly, Mr Horace." Caromel began to purr in a deep-throated rumble that was almost a growl. "I've always had a fancy to go adventuring, but I've never had the chance before. The Wisest One needs me too much. She said I could go this time, though, because I'm clever." She twirled a long white whisker. "Not to put too fine a point on it, Mr Horace, she thought the boy needed help – and she was quite right. I've been watching him, and my last night's dinner would make a better stab at adventuring."

Horace nodded gravely. "Did you see how he was taken in by those two tricksters?"

"Oh, I did!" Caromel chuckled. "Of course, I couldn't show myself. They'd have hunted me high and low until I was caught and popped in a cage." She shivered. "Not a nice thought. But I'll be travelling alongside you from now on, and they do say that two heads are better than one – especially when one of the heads is as clever as I am."

Listening to this made Max uncomfortable. The conversation was reminding him of the way his old school teacher used to talk about him to his parents – as if he was useless.

He slid off the donkey, and faced Caromel.

"Excuse me," he said as firmly as he could. "It's kind of you to offer to help, but I'm sure I can manage on my own."

The big cat sprang neatly onto Horace's back and settled herself comfortably. Now above Max's eye level, she put her head on one side and twinkled at him.

"Butter my paws and twiddle my whiskers. Don't tell me you're going to be a horrid old crosspatch! We can have SUCH a lovely time adventuring together, precious boy. By the way, I hardly like to ask – but have you been using the book the Wisest One gave you?"

Max had forgotten about the book. He pulled it out of his pocket and waved it at Caromel.

"There's nothing in it," he said.

"You can't have been looking properly," Caromel told him, and Max opened it. To his astonishment, there was a picture of the Crimps on the first page. Underneath was written:

These evil folk with foxy smiles
Have caught you with their cunning wiles!

Max hurriedly turned the page, but the rest of the book was just as empty as it had been before.

"That's no help," he said indignantly. "It tells me what's already happened. I need to know what happens next!"

Caromel stretched out a large furry paw, and inspected it. "Hmm … that's as may be. Sometimes it's best not to know too much about the future, sweetie. Leads to nervousness and wobbles. But standing here chit-chatting won't get us across those Hungry Marshes, and I really do want to see those giants. Of course, I'm relying on you to get us to the other side. If there's one thing I absolutely HATE, it's getting my paws wet! Mr Horace, do let's go."

Unable to think of any answer, Max found himself walking along beside the donkey and the enormous cat.

Gradually the unpleasant suspicion that he was regarded as a failure by his fellow travellers faded away and, by the time they came to the end of the path and saw the expanse of grey-brown marshland in front of them, he was almost cheerful. Pools of water caught the sunlight and gleamed gold, and creamy white water lilies floated peacefully on the surface; tall green rushes edged the pools as if they were keeping guard, and Max thought it looked more beautiful than frightening.

"When do I start telling stories—" he began, but he was interrupted by the marsh itself. The tufts of grass and clumps of tall reeds began to move. First they heaved up, then they heaved down, and then they swayed gently from side to side … and every time they moved there was a glutinous squelching noise, as if an enormous animal was licking its lips and belching in preparation for a delicious meal.

"If you're asking my opinion, I'd suggest you start right now. If not sooner," Horace said. He was

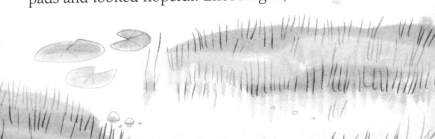

staring at the marsh, where a faint green mist was rising. Tendrils curled towards the travellers and an unpleasant odour of rotting vegetation came with it.

Max swallowed hard and tried to think of a story, any story, but the mist seemed to have crept into his mind. He could think of nothing.

"ATISHOO!" Caromel sneezed loudly, and as Max jumped a story popped up in his head.

"Once upon a time," he said, "there were three little pigs…"

As he spoke the mist reared up, then sank back into the marsh. The squelching noises faded and were replaced by a whispered, "Sssssssssh…" as a breeze came wandering in and out of the reeds and rushes. A couple of frogs hopped onto the lily pads and looked hopeful. Encouraged, Max went on with his story. Behind him Caromel began to purr, but Horace grunted crossly.

"Don't just stand there! We're not here as entertainment – look for a way through."

Taken by surprise, Max lost his thread. The second little pig was suddenly in danger of meeting a man carrying bricks instead of sticks as Max hesitated, and the mist rose up like a warning.

Max gulped, apologized and looked wildly to left and right. Seeing no sign of any walkway, he stepped out onto the edge of the marsh, fully expecting to sink … but although dark water oozed on either side, the ground was surprisingly firm beneath his feet.

He went on walking and Horace followed carefully behind him. Caromel, still perched on the saddle, was listening to the story with every appearance of enjoyment.

When the Big Bad Wolf threatened to blow the brick house down, she whispered, "Be careful! Don't let him in, you foolish little pigs!"

The story of The Three Little Pigs was followed by Jack and the Beanstalk. By the time Max had brought Jack safely down the Beanstalk, they were halfway across the marshy ground and he could see the strange rocky landscape on the other side.

The Hungry Marshes were bubbling contentedly all around him, his feet were still finding firm ground, and he rattled happily through Cinderella.

When the story ended Caromel sighed in satisfaction. "The Wisest One used to tell me that one. What's next?" She put her head on one side. "A story about a clever cat, perhaps?"

Max, reminded of the story of Puss in Boots, began confidently, but after a few minutes he discovered he couldn't remember what happened after Puss and the miller's son had left home. As he paused, the mist began to swirl about him and his feet began to squelch in an ominous fashion.

Panic made him stutter. "I can't – that is – I don't know what's next—"

A heavy weight landed on his shoulders and warm fur brushed his ear.

"They walk and they walk," Caromel prompted. "And the cat catches a rabbit, which he takes to the king…"

"Oh, yes!" Relief swept over Max.

With Caromel's help he was able to finish the story and the mists sank back, but they hadn't entirely gone. They were lurking, as if they were waiting for him to make another mistake.

Although he was able to keep walking, there was no doubt that the ground was softer. He could hear Horace muttering darkly as his hooves sank at every step – and nervousness made Max speak faster and faster until he was almost gabbling.

"Go slower!" Caromel hissed in his ear. "It's not far now. Go slowly. Describe the king's clothes, sweetie! You know … rubies and diamonds, and all that kind of thing."

Max took a deep breath and did as he was told. "The king had twelve ruby buttons on his coat and three more ruby buttons on his coat sleeves…"

"Very good," the big cat purred. "Keep going!"

Trying his hardest to keep calm, Max listed every type of button he could think of. In his version of the story the king had four diamond buttons on his vest, seven golden buttons on his boots and six emerald buttons on his socks.

He was just wondering if it would be rude to mention the two silver buttons on the king's knickers, when Horace gave an excited snort.

"Oh, bless my humble hooves! I do believe we've done it! I'm walking on hard ground—" The donkey stopped and his eyes bulged as he looked ahead.

"Don't panic, anyone … but I can see GIANTS!"

Chapter Ten

Hamfreda and her grandfather had been arguing for at least half an hour. Glom was more and more determined that the Glommet Six could take to the skies if they could only find a suitable cliff from which to take off; Hamfreda was equally determined that they should stay on the ground.

They were still arguing as they rolled down towards the Hungry Marshes, and only a series of warning squawks from the geese saved them from rolling right in.

They stopped with a jolt, looked up … and then froze.

Right in front of them were three little figures: a
boy, a donkey and a cat.

"LOOK!" Hamfreda was shouting in her
excitement. "Do look, Gramps! They're so SMALL!"

King Glom took no notice. He was struggling
with the braking system and muttering to himself.

The travellers, however, reeled back in alarm.
Max clapped his hands to his ears, Caromel arched

her back and hissed, and Horace rolled his eyes
and showed his teeth.

Hamfreda, assuming Max was greeting her and
not wishing to be rude, put her hands over her own
ears before extricating herself from the cockpit of
the Glommet Six.

"Some kind of strange tradition," she told herself.

Max took a deep breath and bowed, even though his heart was pounding and his mouth dry. In spite of all the books he had read, he was still shocked by how large the giants were. King Glom, tinkering with the mechanics inside his flying machine, was a mountainous figure; Hamfreda was twice his size, and the geese were as tall as Horace.

"How do you do?" he said. "Might I introduce myself? I'm Prince Maximilian."

Hamfreda grinned at him. "I'm Hamfreda, and that's my grandfather over in that contraption. He's King Glom." She put her head on one side. "Did you say you were a prince?"

Max nodded. "Oh. Um … yes. And you're a princess?"

Hamfreda threw back her head and roared with laughter, and her laughter was so loud that Max was forced to cover his ears for a second time.

"Oh, Prince Maximilian! I don't think anyone can be called a princess when they haven't had a square meal for weeks, because there's not so much as a scrap of gold *anywhere*, and they're forced to try and save the kingdom single-handed…"

"No gold?" Max went pale. "I thought – that is, my mother told me that you had so much gold you even had gold teapots."

"Gold teapots?" Hamfreda chuckled. "They're ancient history. My grandmother had one, I believe, but it was melted down long before I was born." She studied Max. "It must be wonderful to be your size. So much cheaper! I bet your kingdom has loads of money. We're broke."

As Max's hopes and dreams tumbled round his ears, he did his best to look sympathetic.

Horace, however, had not been trained to be polite and he gave a loud and mocking *heehaw*. "So much for fame and fortune. Sounds as if they're as badly off as you, young man."

"Ooh! Your pet can talk!" Hamfreda, beaming with excitement, thumped towards Horace.

The donkey took one look at her, muttered, "Pet! PET? I'm nobody's pet!" and turned his back.

But Caromel, who had recovered from her fright, leapt down from the prince's shoulders.

"Greetings," she said. "I'm Caromel. My friend here—" she waved a spotty paw towards Max— "forgot to introduce us. He's very new to adventuring, and he doesn't know the rules yet."

"Ooh!" Hamfreda squatted down so she could see Caromel more easily. "I didn't know there were rules. Me and Gramps, we've never left Golden Hollow before. Do you live near here?"

"We've come across the Hungry Marshes." Caromel twirled a whisker. "Our success, of course, was entirely due to me."

"You came across the Hungry Marshes?" Hamfreda's eyes widened and she looked at Max. "Oh, please tell me … have you seen any Papparelli roots?"

Max looked blank. "What are they?"

"They're the roots of Papparelli plants," Hamfreda told him. "We've grown them for hundreds of years in a special tank near our castle, but the tank sprang a leak … and because we couldn't pay the plumber to mend it, the water gradually oozed away and all the plants died."

"What do the roots look like?" Max asked.

"All slimy and twirly," Hamfreda said. "And the leaves look just like waterweed, but bigger. They smell like old socks and they give you pimples."

"Old socks?" Horace swung round and looked at Hamfreda. "Did you say, old socks and pimples?"

"Dear little donkey, it's so terribly cute that you can talk," said Hamfreda. She put out an enormous hand to pat his nose; Horace snorted loudly and swerved away.

"If there's one thing I'm not," he said crossly, "it's cute."

"But you are!" The giant blew him a kiss. "You're the cutest thing I've ever seen! So much nicer than a little fluffy kitten."

Horace, totally outraged, glared at her. "Excuse me, Madam! No kitten has ever had a brain like mine – I've never been so insulted. Never!"

And he stamped away to the shelter of a clump of trees, muttering darkly as he went.

Hoping Hamfreda wouldn't be offended by the donkey's rudeness, Max asked, "So is that why you've come here? To look for roots?"

Hamfreda nodded. "Gramps' *Book of Really Useful Things* says that they grow in marshes and this is the only marsh we know. We need them for the geese… That's what they eat."

Caromel looked superior. "That's nonsense, you know. The Wisest One has a couple of geese and they eat almost everything."

"But these are special geese." Hamfreda sighed.

"Very special. They only eat Papparelli roots and if they don't get the roots they don't lay—"

"Harrumph!" Glom, with some effort, had climbed out of the Glommet Six and now he interrupted his granddaughter. "Hamfreda! Have you seen my glasses? I can't find them anywhere."

"They're on your head, Gramps," Hamfreda told him. She turned back to Max. "As I was saying, we need the roots—"

"HARRUMPH!"

Glom's interruption was even louder. He had put on his glasses and was peering down at Max.

"Be quiet, Hamfreda! Don't you know what you're talking to? That's a human. Didn't they warn you about humans in school?"

"But I don't go to school!" His granddaughter sounded irritated. "You wouldn't let me, remember? You said you could teach me everything I needed to know."

"Oh." Glom scratched his beard. "So I did. Well, I'm teaching you something now. This is a human!

And the important thing to remember is that all humans are greedy. They used to keep coming to try and steal from us … and *that*, Hamfreda, is why our ancestors created the Hungry Marshes and built our homes in Golden Hollow."

"I'm sure Max isn't greedy," Hamfreda said. She turned to Max. "You're not, are you?"

To her astonishment Max blushed. "I'm rather afraid I might be," he said slowly. "I did come here to look for gold. My father's kingdom has run out of money, and we hoped you might be able to help. I didn't know you were as hard up as us. I'm sorry."

Glom snorted. "Just as I thought! Hamfreda, come away at once. And you, you horrid little human, go back to where you came from and take those animals with you. I hope you sink in the Hungry Marshes— JUST A MINUTE." Glom stopped and stared at Max. "Why, in the name of Glom the Great, didn't you get gulped and gobbled on the way over? Everyone else does."

Caromel nodded. "Glug, glug, glug. And BURP!"

"I told the marshes stories," Max said, and he shivered. "It was scary."

"Stories?" Glom's bristly eyebrows rose. "What do you mean *stories*?"

"Cinderella, Puss in Boots … those kind of stories. The Wisest One told me the Hungry Marshes like them." A thought came to Max and he added, "I'm sure the Wisest One could tell you where to find Papparelli roots. She knows almost everything."

Caromel pranced round Glom's enormous ankles. "The boy's wrong, as usual, your Royal Giantness. The Wisest One knows EVERYTHING!"

"Did you hear that, Gramps?" Hamfreda was excited, but her grandfather frowned.

"How do we know that's not another story?"

Max stood up very straight. "You have the word of Prince Maximilian Olivier Adolphus de Frogholme."

A sudden eager light shone in Glom's eyes. "Would the Wisest One know how to make a flying machine fly?"

"What?" Max stared and Hamfreda sighed.

"That's all Gramps really wants to do," she explained. "He only wants to find the Papparelli roots so I can buy him a trumpet." Seeing Max's bewildered face, she went on, "He thinks the trumpet will help him get the Glommet Ten into the air."

Wondering if Hamfreda and her grandfather were more than a little mad, Max asked, "But I still don't understand. How will roots help you buy a trumpet?"

There was a sudden roar from Glom. "He doesn't know! He doesn't know about the geese!" The giant punched the air and stomped round in a circle, making the ground shake under Max's feet. "You, human! What do geese lay?"

Max was beginning to feel nervous. The King of the Giants was definitely mad. "Eggs," he said.

"But what KIND of eggs?"

"Erm … goose eggs." Max looked over his shoulder wondering how quickly he, Horace and Caromel could get away. "Bigger than hen's eggs. Probably just as boring. If you'll excuse me, I think we ought to be going…"

"WAIT!" Glom sat down with a thump. "Listen to me, human. You go back to this Wisest One. Ask her what I'm doing wrong. If you bring me the answer, I'll – I'll give you one of my geese."

He leant forward. His face was so near to Max that the boy could see the whiskers in his nose.

"And that goose, my little human, will bring you your gold."

Max, thinking he couldn't have heard properly, looked at Hamfreda. "What does he mean?"

Hamfreda, half-laughing and half-frowning, said, "It's true. The geese lay golden eggs … but only if they eat Papparelli roots, so you'll need to find some of those before your goose is any good to you. It's not much of a bargain."

"Oh. I mean, thank you – thank you very much." Max's mind was whirling. A goose that laid golden eggs? Surely that would solve all his parents' problems. If he went to see the Wisest One and asked her where to find the roots, why, surely she would know the answer. She knew the answer to everything. Caromel had said so.

He bowed low, and Glom peered at him.

"So do we have a deal, human? You'll ask about my flying machine?"

"And the roots," Hamfreda added. "Don't forget the roots!"

Max bowed again. "You have my word."

"Good!" Glom beamed at him. "Now I'm going to sort out the brakes." A thoughtful expression floated over his face. "And while I'm at it, I might as well check the floatability. And the wings."

"What?" Hamfreda gave him a suspicious look. "Why would you check the wings?"

Her grandfather pretended not to hear. Whistling innocently, he turned his back and climbed into the Glommet Six.

Hamfreda shook her head. "He's up to something, I know he is." She sighed. "I'd love to come with you but I just can't trust him."

"We'll be back as soon as we can," Max promised and the geese all hissed as if they were encouraging him in his task.

Chapter Eleven

On the other side of the Hungry Marshes, just beyond the village of Nether Dread, Mr and Mrs Crimp were discussing the best way to kidnap Max.

Mrs Crimp was enthusing about the simple method of putting a bag over his head, but Mr Crimp thought it would be better to dig a hole, cover it with leaves and wait for the prince to fall in.

"That way," he explained, "there's no danger of that mean-minded donkey running away with him again. The donkey will fall in too."

Mrs Crimp considered this, her head on one side. "It'll have to be a very big hole ... and we don't have a spade."

"True." Mr Crimp nodded. "Do we have a bag?"

"I'm not sure." Mrs Crimp dug around in her wheelbarrow, and came up smiling her widest crocodile smile. "Look! We've not only got a lovely big bag, we've got oodles and oodles of rope. We could tie it across the path, then when the donkey trips over the prince will fall off—"

"And we'll drop the bag over his head—"

"And chuck him in the wheelbarrow—"

"And take him – where?" Mr Crimp looked blank.

"To the shack in the woods?" Mrs Crimp suggested.

"To the shack in the woods," Mr Crimp agreed.

Mrs Crimp rubbed her hands in glee. "And then we'll write our letter to the palace and ask for – how much shall we ask for, Crimpie?"

Mr Crimp's eyes gleamed. "A hundred pieces of gold?"

"Goodness me, Crimpie, this is a prince! Five hundred pieces at least."

"Done." And Mr Crimp and Mrs Crimp shook hands.

If Mr and Mrs Crimp could have seen King Ferdinand and Queen Gloria at that precise moment, they would have made very different plans.

Max's parents were staring at the chickens in the castle yard, and wondering if there was any chance that they might lay a couple of eggs for their tea. The cupboards were empty and so were their stomachs.

"You could sing to them, dear," the queen suggested. "I've heard that can be helpful."

The king snorted. "More likely to make them go on strike."

"Maybe a rousing chorus of the national anthem might do the trick," the queen said hopefully. "It should remind them of their duty."

"Duty?" The king snorted again, then paused. "What's that smell?"

"Smell, dear?" The queen sniffed the air. "Oh, that's the moat! It's those waterweeds. Ever since the gardener left there's been no one to pull them out, and they're getting worse and worse. Would you like a clothes peg for your nose? I find that an excellent solution if I have to go over the bridge."

King Ferdinand frowned. "They must be cleared away at once!" He scratched at his ear. "Now I come to think about it, that greengrocer chap complained about the smell. Said it gave him pimples … AHA!"

The queen raised her eyebrows. "Have you had an idea, dear?"

"Indeed I have!" The king puffed out his chest. "I shall order the greengrocer to help me clear the moat this very day. He made a ridiculous bargain over the use of his donkey. Asked for far too much! But it proves he's greedy so I shall offer him another couple of gold pieces in return for his services.

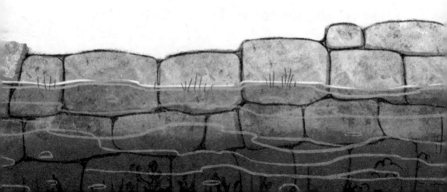

When Maximilian returns the moat will be clean,
and every last twist of weed will be gone."

"How lovely, dear," the queen said. She peered at
a small brown chicken. "Do you think she might be
about to lay an egg?"

"I've no time for that now," the king said. "I'm off
to see the greengrocer!"

And half an hour later the greengrocer could
be seen marching towards the moat armed with a
bucket and a spade – having successfully bargained
for another *five* gold pieces.

The sun was sinking and a cold wind had begun
to blow, as Max and Caromel walked towards the
Hungry Marshes for their return journey. Horace,
chewing a thistle, came too, but only after Max had
been to fetch him from under the trees.

"About time too," he said. "And if you take my advice, you'll never come here again." He flattened his ears and showed his teeth. "Nicer than a kitten! The cutest thing she's ever seen! I didn't agree to go adventuring in order to be demeaned and insulted. *Heehaw!*"

"I think she meant it nicely," Max suggested, but Horace snorted angrily.

"Nicely? What's nice about an insult? Taking her side, are you? Typical! Two legs against four legs, same as always. There's no fairness in this life, no fairness at all."

Caromel was studying the darkening sky. "Do let's be quick, sweetie," she said. "Have you thought of lots of stories? I really don't want to get my dear little paws wet … although of course I'll be riding across the marshes."

Max saw that she was shivering. A thought came to him and he took off the cloak his mother had given him.

"Here," he said, "Why don't you wear this?"

"Huh!" Horace grunted disapprovingly. "That'll make you a walking sideshow and no mistake."

Caromel, however, purred with pleasure. "Delightful, sweetie," she said, and leapt up onto Horace's back. Max handed her the cloak and she wrapped it round her shoulders and sat up very straight. "I was born for finery such as this," she announced. "My ancestors were royal, you know. All I need now is a crown."

With a grin, Max handed her his and she took it graciously before giving it a curious look.

"Ahem! Sweetie, were you aware that this is nothing more than tin? And cheap tin at that!"

"I know." Max shrugged. "All our gold crowns were melted down ages ago to pay the bills. Actually, I prefer the tin sort. They're much lighter and it doesn't matter so much if you lose them."

Caromel placed the crown on her head and smoothed her whiskers. "I see what you mean. Splendidly comfortable. And it fits as if it were made for me."

Max didn't answer. He had pulled the Wisest
One's book out of his pocket and was frowning.

Be sure that every deed is true
Or nothing good will come to you.

"I do wish it was more encouraging," he said.
Horace gave a hollow laugh.

"And why should it be? You haven't exactly
covered yourself in glory so far… You've met the
giants, and they're as poor as you are. Do as I say:
go home, and forget about this adventuring. Why
should you help that giant? Totally unappreciative

of the unique and exceptional, even when it's right under her nose."

"But I have to help her!" Max told him. "If I can find the roots, the giant king is going to give me a goose of my very own."

"Huh!" Horace was unimpressed. "All skin and bone. Won't make you much of a dinner."

"But you don't understand," Max said earnestly. "Those geese lay golden eggs – we'd be rich. Really, truly, properly rich!"

The donkey didn't answer. He stared, coughed, twitched his ears and coughed again. Max, more interested to see if the book had any more advice for him, turned the page and read out loud:

Trust yourself. Although you roam
The answer may be close to home.
Honour is not guaranteed –
A friend may hide the help you need.

"What on earth does that mean?" he said.

"HEEHAW!"

Astonishing both Max and Caromel, Horace skittered sideways and rolled his eyes wildly.

"Don't ask me! I'm only a donkey, remember. I don't know anything about anything, do I? Nothing at all! Brain like a little fluffy kitten, remember. One more brain cell and I'd be a log of wood! Absolutely – no doubt about it."

Remembering how opinionated Horace usually was, Max looked at him in astonishment.

Caromel sniffed. "That doesn't sound like you, Mr Horace."

"Doesn't sound like me? I am what I am. A mere donkey, beast of burden, four legs and covered in fur… What more do you want? Singing? Dancing? Walking on a tightrope in a little pink tutu?"

Max took off his spectacles, wiped them on the edge of his tunic and put them on again. Horace was obviously upset about something – but what?

"Have I done something wrong?" he asked.

"You? Oh no. No, no, no, no, no." The donkey gave a hollow laugh. "When a vastly oversized stranger calls me names, do you defend me? Explain what a worthy companion I've been, carrying you all the way to the land of giants, let alone single-handedly saving you from a pair of double-crossing pranksters? Oh no. Am I thanked? Appreciated? Never. Royalty, it would appear, has no loyalty. But, hey, forget I said anything. What do my feelings matter? Let's head for that marsh and hope it's not feeling too hungry."

Mystified by Horace's speech, Max decided it was best to ignore it. "Let's go."

Caromel nodded. "Onward, my sweeties! And don't you worry, dear boy. Should you falter, I have many stories at my whiskers' ends."

Max, trying hard not to resent the big cat's patronizing tone, said, "Thank you," and stepped out into the marsh. "I'm going to begin with The Billy Goats Gruff."

Chapter Twelve

As Max began his story there was a quivering over the marsh and a faint murmur, as if it approved of Max's choice. Remembering his panic on the first journey, he took the story slowly and added lots of detail. Each of the billy goats was described from the top of their horns to the tip of their hooves and given a complicated set of clothes to wear. The marsh seemed to particularly appreciate the troll and quivered in delight every time Max sang, "I'm a troll! Rol-de-rol … I'm going to eat you for dinner!"

Caromel, sitting very upright on Horace's back, stretched out a furry paw and inspected her nails.

"I expect it's thinking how much it would like to eat *us* for dinner," she remarked.

Max felt a surge of anxiety and almost forgot where he had got to. With an effort he went back to the story, and the great big billy goat gruff finally tramped over the bridge and tossed the troll into the river. The marsh gave a loud belch of satisfaction and Max, after a moment's thought, began the story of The Princess and the Frog. This too seemed to be a satisfactory choice, and the ground stayed comfortably solid under Max's feet.

As they neared the other side and the ground grew firmer, Horace grew more and more subdued. When Caromel asked him if he was enjoying his adventures, he merely grunted – and when she suggested he was tired, he didn't answer at all.

"Are you being a bit of an old grumpy-drawers, sweetie?" she asked, but there was still no response and the big cat raised her eyebrows. "Sorry I spoke,

I'm sure." She turned to Max. "Our Mr Horace has something on his mind, wouldn't you say?"

"HEEHAW!" Horace gave an angry bray, then burst into a gallop. Caromel held on grimly to the saddle and Max, puffing, ran after them.

"Please … slow … down!" he panted. "I can't … go … as fast … as you!"

Horace took no notice and bounded out of the marshes and onto the shore. It was nearly dark, but the road to Nether Dread was clearly marked and Horace continued at a canter, ignoring Max. Max did his best to catch up, but he was tired and the gap between him and the donkey quickly widened.

Caromel, still perched on the saddle with the cloak swirled over her shoulders and the crown at a rakish angle, seemed to be enjoying the ride. Max was almost sure that he had heard her say, "Yee-ha!" as Horace took off.

So much for Caromel helping me on my adventures, he thought bitterly. *At this rate I'll be left on my own and I'm not sure I know the way to—*

"HEEHAW! HEEHAW! HEEHAW!"

Max stared.

Horace had fallen over and a tall, thin figure, only just visible in the late evening light, leapt out from the bushes. With a shout of triumph it pounced on Caromel and, as Max's eyes grew wider and wider, an enormous bag dropped down from the trees above and engulfed the big cat.

A shorter, stouter figure followed the bag, pulled the cord tight, then danced round it in a circle.

Caromel twisted and wriggled and screeched, but she was unable to escape. A moment later she was a writhing bundle on the shoulder of the tall, thin figure.

"Don't wriggle, Your Highness, it won't do you any good," The voice was familiar, and Max gasped.

"That's Mr Crimp! And … and he thinks that he's caught ME." He crouched down, and began to creep closer, listening as he went.

"I'll tie up the donkey, Crimpie dear." It was Mrs Crimp. Max saw her stomp across to Horace, who was still lying on the ground and moaning. In two minutes he was trussed up like a turkey, the rope wound round and round him.

When he let out a protesting "HEEHAW!" she threw her scarf over his head and laughed triumphantly as she tied it tightly.

"Got him! And we've got the boy too."

"Oh no you haven't," Max muttered, and he clenched his fists. "And I'll make sure you never do!"

But even as Max tried his best to believe that he could be a brave adventurer, Mrs Crimp wheeled the wheelbarrow out from under a bush and dumped Caromel inside.

"And now for the donkey!" Mr Crimp came to join his wife and, between them, they heaved Horace alongside Caromel. Mr Crimp began to wheel it away and Mrs Crimp followed him, talking loudly as they set off into the woods. She seemed nervous. Although there was a lantern tied to the

wheelbarrow, she kept peering into the darkness as if she expected monsters to jump out at any moment.

"It's so very, very dark out there, Crimpie … and I'm sure I saw something moving. A bear? Could it be a bear? Or a wolf?"

Mr Crimp grunted. The barrow was heavy, and he was only able to go slowly. "Don't be foolish, Mrs Crimp. There aren't any bears, or wolves. Think about the gold instead!"

"Oh, yes, Crimpie dear! You're right. I'll try and think about the gold. When shall we send the letter to the palace? Five hundred gold pieces … or they never see their itsy bitsy little boy again!"

Chapter Thirteen

Hamfreda was bored. The sun had set and it was dark, with heavy clouds covering the moon. Glom had completed his adjustments, whatever they were, and was now snoring loudly – Hamfreda suspected that he would stay asleep until morning. He was comfortably sprawled over both seats with his feet on the steering wheel.

The geese were sleeping too, but every so often one of them would wake and fix Hamfreda with a reproachful eye. Their gaze made her feel uncomfortable and she began to walk round and round the Glommet Six.

A brief gap in the clouds allowed the moon to shine through for a moment, and something glittered by the steering wheel. Hamfreda looked, looked again – and pounced.

"There's a key! And keys turn things on: it must be important."

Holding her breath, she quietly slid the key out and dropped it into her pocket.

"There! That'll keep Gramps safe."

"*Hiss?*" One of the geese was standing beside her, and Hamfreda glanced down and smiled.

"Gramps always says, look out for others. I'm going to help Max." She folded her arms. "If he can tell stories and get across, so can I. You stay here, and hopefully I'll come back knowing exactly where to find your dinners!"

The goose ducked her head and hissed loudly, and at once her companions woke up and hissed a reply. Next minute they were all out of the Glommet Six, lining up behind Hamfreda. "*HISS!*"

"You want to come too?" the giant asked.

The geese nodded, and Hamfreda made her decision. "All right. But make sure you keep very close to me. These aren't ordinary marshes … they're hungry. Hungry for stories … and for anyone trying to get to the other side!" And, remembering Max's instructions, she strode into the marshes shouting, "Once upon a time there was a shoemaker, and he and his wife made shoes but nobody bought them…"

The marsh shivered: Hamfreda was on her way, the geese close behind her. Sometimes she hesitated and the marsh mist rose ominously, but as she found her voice again the mist faded.

At last she reached the other side and squelched onto the shore, the geese following in her wake. The clouds were beginning to clear and there was enough moonlight to see the new land she had come to.

Hamfreda looked about with interest. The size of the signpost made her laugh and a stray cat running across the road made her catch her breath. "It's so TINY!" The geese waddled over, and the cat gave a terrified screech and fled.

"And now to find Max," Hamfreda told herself. "At least there's only one road. I can't go too far wrong."

She began to walk; the sound of her footsteps on the cobbles echoed in the cold night air, and she took to the grass verge in order to move more silently. The geese pattered along behind her, occasionally giving a mournful honk.

"Oh!" Hamfreda's eyes grew round as saucers as she saw Mr Crimp's horse tied to a tree. "A teeny tiny horse! Such a ducky little thing. Can you talk? Would you like a cuddle?"

But the horse had never seen a giant before. Ears back, he reared up, broke his reins and dashed away up the road.

Hamfreda sighed. "I only wanted to pat it," she said sadly. She was about to go back when something caught her eye.

It was Max! He was leaning against a tree and frowning into the woods. Hamfreda tiptoed up, and was about to shout "Boo!" when he turned.

"Hamfreda!" He put his finger to his lips. "It's Caromel and Horace – they've been kidnapped!"

"Kidnapped?" Hamfreda looked blank.

Max nodded. "These horrible people, Mr and Mrs Crimp, they think it's *me* that they've caught, and they're going to blackmail my parents. They think they're rich." Max gulped as he thought about Mrs Crimp's threats. His parents didn't have one gold piece, let alone five hundred. "I'm going to have to stop them and rescue Caromel and Horace."

Having Hamfreda beside him made him feel much braver. He took off his spectacles, rubbed them clean, then put them back on again with a determined push of his thumb.

"I'm going to follow the Crimps and see where they're going. When the clouds clear, I can just see the tracks of the wheelbarrow."

Hamfreda bent down to see, then straightened and looked at the thick forest ahead of her. "I'll clear a path." She gave Max a conspiratorial grin.

"There are advantages to being as big as me, you know."

The wheelbarrow had slowed the Crimps down, and it wasn't long until Max and Hamfreda heard them crashing through the undergrowth.

Cautiously they drew closer, following as silently as they could. Once Hamfreda stepped on a stick and it snapped with an alarming *CRACK*!

Mrs Crimp jumped and squealed, but Mr Crimp told her it was nothing.

"Oops! Sorry!" Hamfreda whispered.

Almost as if they had heard her, the Crimps stopped.

Peering cautiously ahead, Max saw that they were standing outside a wooden shack. He silently pointed it out to Hamfreda who gave him a big thumbs up.

If they shut them in and go away, we can rescue Horace and Caromel, he thought, and it was obvious that Hamfreda was thinking the same … but their hopes were dashed. The wheelbarrow was shoved inside, the door slammed shut and a heavy bar dropped into place.

But then Mr and Mrs Crimp hung the lantern on a branch, took out a packet of sandwiches and a large bottle, and sat themselves down. When he saw the sandwiches Max's stomach rumbled so loudly he was afraid he'd be heard, but the two kidnappers took no notice.

"Delicious, Mrs Crimp!" Mr Crimp remarked. "If there's one thing I like in a sandwich, it's cheese and pickle."

"Just think, Crimpie dear, quite soon we'll be eating off golden plates. And drinking out of golden cups." Mrs Crimp took a long drink. "And we'll never need to sit in a creepy old forest ever again."

Mr Crimp yawned. "You're right, my dear, as you always are. Pass the bottle!"

Chapter Fourteen

Max was studying the shack. He could see by the flickering light of the lantern that it was sturdily made, with walls of roughly cut planks. Might there be a window on the other side?

He beckoned to Hamfreda to bend down so he could whisper in her ear. "I'm going to see what's round the back."

She nodded. "I'll hoot like an owl if they move."

Holding his breath, slipping behind first one tree and then another, Max managed to reach his destination without being noticed. It was much darker on the other side, but when he tentatively put out his hand, he could feel cracks between the planks.

He put his mouth to one of the gaps and whispered, "Caromel! Horace! Can you hear me?"

The only response was the sound of breathing and Max's heart fluttered in his chest as he whispered again: "Caromel! Horace! It's me, Max!"

He was rewarded by a rustling, a faint growl and a hissed, "Just let me get at them! I'll teach them to tie me up in a bag. They'll wish they'd never been born by the time I've done with them. Sweetie – is there any way you can untie me?"

Max, with some difficulty, squeezed his hand into a lower crack. "Can you get near the wall?"

There was a rumble and a heaving. Max felt rough canvas under his fingers, but he couldn't reach the rope that tied the bag.

"Move nearer," he instructed. And then he sneezed.

On the other side of the shack Mrs Crimp raised her head. "Did you hear something, Crimpie?"

As Max froze, Hamfreda's owl call came floating eerily through the cold night air. "*Ter whit! Ter wooooooo!*"

Mr Crimp gasped and Mrs Crimp screamed, "Crimpie! It's a ghost! Let's go! Let's get out of here—"

"Nonsense. There's no such things as ghosts." But Mr Crimp's voice was uncertain and Max had an idea.

"Caromel," he whispered, "I'm going to try and untie you, but can you keep very quiet? I'm going to pretend I'm a ghost. They're sure to open the door to check if I'm really dead … and then you can spring out and scare them away!"

There was no answer, and Max was beginning to wonder if she had heard him, when there was a faint breath. "I apologize. You do have a brain, after all."

Deciding to take this as a compliment, Max wriggled his fingers as far as they would go. A splinter made him wince, but at last he found the end of the rope that kept Caromel imprisoned and began to work on the knot. It was difficult. Not only was it pitch dark, but he could only use one hand

and the gap was narrow and uncomfortable. He picked away, but apart from another splinter he made no progress.

"Sweetie … I'm balanced on my tippy toes and I'm getting cramp. Bear with me while I move a little."

There was the sound of canvas brushing against wood and Max's fingers found a different angle on the rope. This, surprisingly, was better. To his delight he felt the knot loosen, then give way.

At once there was a swirl of movement and a soft purr. "A million thanks, sweetie."

"Can you untie Horace? Is he all right?" Max asked anxiously and Caromel chuckled.

"I can do that." She chuckled again. "He's been muttering to himself ever since we got here."

Max moved back from the shack and took a moment to suck his painful finger. Then, with infinite care, he crept back to where Hamfreda was crouched under the drooping branches of a willow tree. She listened intently as he breathed his plan into her ear, before enthusiastically nodding her approval.

The Crimps were arguing
over the last sandwich and the two
watchers were pleased to see that Mrs Crimp
kept glancing nervously over her shoulder.

Mr Crimp also seemed unsettled.

"Wooooooo!" Max called
softly, "Wooooooo!"

"Ooooooh!" Hamfreda
echoed. "Ooooooh!"

The Crimps froze.

"Oh me, oh my, please tell me… Where am I?" Max's voice quavered and shook, and he rustled the branches of the tree. "The time has come for me to leave my mortal body, and to fly…"

Mrs Crimp buried her head in the sandwich bag, but Mr Crimp asked in a trembling voice, "Who are you? What do you want?"

"I am the ghost of Prince Maximilian Olivier Adolphus de Frogholme, done to death in this forest by the hand of—"

Max, who was beginning to enjoy himself hugely, was interrupted by a frantic scream from Mrs Crimp. "It's the boy – that's his voice! Crimpie, we've killed him!"

"Rubbish!" But Mr Crimp sounded far from convinced. "He's playing a trick. Come and look… He'll be tied up, and laughing at us."

And Mr Crimp pulled Mrs Crimp to her feet, put his hand on the heavy wooden beam that kept the door closed, heaved it up …

and was greeted by a spitting, hissing Caromel, who launched herself out of the shack at him in a flurry of spots and stripes. With a piercing scream, the Crimps turned to run – only to see a gigantic figure looming out of the darkness, accompanied by a gaggle of enormous geese that gleamed ghostly white in the moonlight.

"Oooooooh!" the figure wailed. "Oooooooh!"

With another shriek the Crimps spun round
and saw the door of the shack invitingly open
in front of them.

Desperate for safety, with no
time to think what they were
doing, they hurtled inside –
Max slammed the door shut,
and dropped the bar.

"Got them!" he said, and Hamfreda cheered loudly.

"That was fun!"

"The perfect punishment, my sweeties," Caromel agreed. She looked at Hamfreda and raised a paw in greeting. "Sincere thanks are due to both of you. Wouldn't you agree, Mr Horace? Mr Horace! Where are you?"

The bushes rustled and Horace emerged: a sad, dejected and limping Horace.

His only reply was to shake his head.

"What's the matter?" Max asked. "Aren't you pleased to be free?"

Horace heaved an enormous sigh.

"I," he said, "am a wicked and evil animal and I deserve to be made into a rug. Made into a rug and walked over by a thousand dirty feet."

"What?" Max stared him, then at Hamfreda – who shrugged. "What do you mean?"

The donkey sighed again. "I have a secret … a guilty secret that weighs upon my soul."

Max looked at Caromel. "Do you know what he's talking about?"

"No idea, sweetie." Caromel shrugged. "Do explain, Mr Horace."

There was a pause, and then Horace began his confession.

"That giant called me a pet. Called me cute. She insulted me! And you, young man, did you explain how I had been your wise advisor, your constant companion, your saviour? You did not. You said—" an agonized expression crossed Horace's face— "she meant it 'nicely'. So I thought: why should I help to find the stupid roots? Serves you both right, I thought. But now you and your enormous friend have rescued me and coals of fire are heaped upon my unworthy head because I never told you—"

Max was having difficulty hiding his impatience. "Told me WHAT?"

Horace shifted uneasily, coughed, looked down at the ground, coughed again and then said in a rush, "The moat round your castle is stuffed with Papparelli roots. White and wriggly. Smell of old socks. Give people pimples… Can't be anything else."

Max's mouth opened, then shut again. "So – so all we have to do is go home?"

Horace nodded. "Yes."

"And we'll find Papparelli roots in our moat?"

Horace looked irritated. "Ears turned to cloth all of a sudden, have they? Yes. THERE ARE PAPPARELLI ROOTS IN YOUR MOAT."

Max and Hamfreda looked at each other, their eyes sparkling.

"We've found them!" cried Hamfreda, giving Max such a cheery congratulatory slap on the back that he was sent sprawling.

He was laughing as he picked himself up. "We did it!" he crowed, and he hugged as much of Hamfreda as he could reach.

Caromel yawned. "So all's well that end's well, sweetie. Might I suggest we all take time for a little sleep? There's no hurry, and I can see a delightful hollow filled with dry leaves." And without waiting for an answer, she stalked in between the trees and settled herself down. "Do feel free to join me. I don't believe I snore."

Max hesitated. "Shouldn't we get back as quickly as we can?"

Hamfreda sat down with a thump that shook the ground. "My geese could do with a rest." She picked one up. "They've been pitter-pattering a long way. Their poor flat feet are quite worn out!"

Max, with a secret sigh of relief, sank down beside her. He was exhausted, but hadn't wanted to admit it; in the stories he had read, adventurers always carried on despite their aches and pains.

"It'll be much easier to travel by day," he said, "and we'll move faster after a rest…"

A minute later his eyes were closed.

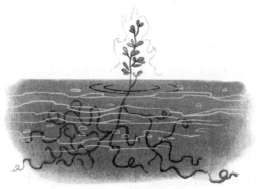

Chapter Fifteen

Back at King Ferdinand's castle, the moat
clearing operation had stopped for the night.
The greengrocer had done well, and there was
already a large pile of twisted white roots heaped
on a patch of grass. He had demanded extra gold
to compensate for the pimples that were beginning
to cover his arms, and the king had unwillingly
agreed. The queen, when she came out to
see how he was progressing, clapped
her hands.

"How lovely! We can have a bonfire!"

The greengrocer looked doubtful. "Best to wait until tomorrow. They're nasty slimy things, those roots. Won't burn unless they dry out a bit."

"Tomorrow, then." The queen beamed. "A celebratory beacon to welcome Prince Maximilian home! Bringing with him golden teapots, galore!"

The greengrocer's face brightened. "I'll be back bright and early to finish the job, Ma'am."

The greengrocer wasn't the only one to make an early start the following morning. A strange procession made its way out of the woods and onto the road that led to Nether Dread. Led by a prince with leaves in his hair, it consisted of a large cat-like creature riding on a donkey, a giant and seven white geese.

The giant had a large bag on her back that alternatively threatened and whined. Max had decided that it would be wrong to leave Mr and Mrs Crimp shut up in the wooden shack, and Hamfreda had volunteered to look after them.

"They're quite cute as long as you don't listen to them." She gave Horace a wistful look. "Not nearly as cute as a dear little donkey, of course … but they'll improve with training." She gave the bag a sharp shake. "Be quiet!"

Max grinned, despite his hunger. Breakfast had been a few berries and the leftover crusts from Mrs Crimp's sandwiches; shared with a hungry giant and a large cat, these had been far from enough. He hadn't slept well, either. Caromel's sleepy purrs had been worse than any snoring, and Max had managed nothing more than an intermittent doze.

Horace was the only one who had eaten an adequate meal. He had found a large patch of thistles, and enjoyed himself enormously. Having shed his burden of guilt he was almost happy, and walked briskly along the road, looking to left and right as if he'd never been that way before.

Max was thinking as he walked along. He had looked in his book that morning, and had been pleased to read:

> **Hungry Marshes safely crossed,**
> **Now to seek what you have lost.**

That'll be the Papparelli roots, he thought. *Fancy them being in our moat all along … and we never knew what they were!*

He looked at Caromel.

"Should we go and visit the Wisest One first, do you think? Or go and get the roots?"

Caromel licked her paw. "Ask your book, sweetie."

Max opened the book again.

Look ahead to future visions!
Time to make your own decisions.

_Oh!_ Max stuffed the book back in his pocket without reading it out loud. _What vision do I have for the future? Enough money to pay the bills ... so we ought to get the geese fed as soon as possible._

Turning round, he inspected the royal geese. It had been so dark the night before, he had only noticed how tall they were; now, he realized they were desperately thin.

Hamfreda saw him looking, and nodded.

"They won't last much longer. I don't suppose you could carry one or two? Just to give them a rest?" She scooped up a couple of geese and tucked them under her arms.

"Of course," Max said and he bent to pick up one of the geese.

She was heavier than he had expected, but he managed to struggle upright. The goose gave a grateful sigh and laid her head on his shoulder.

"She likes you," Hamfreda told him. "That's Violet. You'd better have her as your present from Gramps. Isn't she just a cutesy pie?"

Max wasn't entirely sure he agreed. He could only

just get his arms round her body, thin as she was, and his shoulders were already aching.

On and on they travelled. Max's back hurt, his arms had lost all feeling and Violet seemed to get heavier at every step. None of the geese would go near Caromel, and while Horace grumpily agreed to carry the smallest goose she didn't look comfortable and flapped down after only half a mile.

"We should have brought the wheelbarrow," Max said. He tried to hide a sigh. "We've only just got past Nether Dread … it's miles to go yet."

Hamfreda was looking at the line of geese behind her. Several were limping and, as she watched, one lay down and closed its eyes.

"Oh dear," she said. "I don't suppose you could carry another?" Max was about to answer when a strange thumping sound behind him made him swing round. Hamfreda turned to look as well – and gasped. "Gramps! It's Gramps!"

The Glommet Six was powering towards them, a red-faced King Glom peddling for all he was worth.

The geese cackled and scattered as he came to a halt, and Hamfreda ran over to him.

"Gramps! How did you get here? And…" she blushed. "How did you get moving without the key?"

"Key? What key? Oh, that key. Never use it." Her grandfather sounded extremely pleased with himself. "This little beauty runs on pedal power. Guess what, Hamfreda? I got her up in the air! I flew! Only a few feet up … and it needed a jolly good run before she took off, but I flew over the Hungry Marshes!"

His hair was standing straight up on end with excitement.

"A crash landing, but nothing broken. Have you found those roots yet? I want to buy more wood. I'm going to build the Glommet Six Plus – and then the world will be mine!"

"We know where there are loads of roots," Hamfreda told him. "Max's castle moat is full of them. Can you help us get there?" She pointed to the geese. "They're so hungry they can hardly walk."

Her grandfather nodded. "Hop aboard! The more the merrier."

It took quite a while to squeeze Hamfreda, Max and the geese inside the Glommet Six. Caromel and Horace, much to Horace's indignation, were invited to seat themselves in the rickety basket on wheels that made do as a trailer.

Finally everyone was settled, and the Glommet Six began to move.

"Once … we … get … going," Glom puffed, "we … can … get … a … bit … of … speed … up!"

Max, profoundly grateful that he didn't have to walk for several more miles carrying a heavy goose, grinned. "Don't worry. The moat won't disappear – it will still be there when we arrive."

Chapter Sixteen

"That's better." King Ferdinand folded his arms, and gazed approvingly at the sparkling water.

The queen nodded. "So much nicer, dear. We're just about to have a glorious bonfire and burn all those horrid roots. The greengrocer's lighting it right now. Perhaps we could bake potatoes in the ashes and have a lovely little picnic. What do you think?"

"We'd need some potatoes first," the king pointed out and the queen sighed.

"I do hope our boy comes home soon." She sighed again. "Never mind about the gold. I miss him."

TOOT! TOOT!

The king and queen jumped, then clutched each other as the enormous Glommet Six came rolling up the driveway.

"Help – HELP!" King Ferdinand was pale and shaking. "Call the guard, call the army, call … call anybody. We're being invaded!"

The huge machine shuddered and slowed. Before it had properly ground to a halt, Max had jumped out and was running towards his parents.

"Ma! Pa! It's the best news ever: I've got my very own goose that lays golden—"

He stopped … then yelled, "NOOOOOOOO!" as he saw the clean, clear water shining in the sunshine. "NOOOOOOOO!"

He fell on his knees, his head in his hands.

His parents gazed at him in horror.

"Maximilian!" said the queen. "Whatever is it? What's wrong?"

When Max looked up, there were tears in his eyes. "Why? Why did you clear the moat? WHY? We could have been rich – but we never will be, now."

The queen blinked. "But Maximilian, it was simply stuffed full of horrid weeds!"

"They weren't weeds!" Max shook his fists in agony. "They were Papparelli plants!"

"What? Never heard of them." The king was still very pale. "And never mind the moat. I think – I think – I *think* I can see a GIANT!"

"A giant?" Max turned to see what his father was staring at. "Oh, yes. Pa, meet Glom – the King of the Giants. And Princess Hamfreda, his granddaughter. But, Pa … do you realize what you've done? We've come all this way for just one thing: the Papparelli roots! And you…" He swallowed hard to stop himself from bursting into tears. "You've chucked them away, and—"

Max was suddenly silent. Something was happening behind him; he swung round to look.

HISSSSSSSSSS!

First one goose, then another, and another, and another, and *another* flapped out of the Glommet Six, their eyes gleaming.

Max straightened up, King Ferdinand's mouth dropped open and Queen Gloria stared.

"HISSSSSSSSSS!" The geese began to waddle faster and faster, wings flapping, their beaks open. Away from the moat and round the bridge … and round the corner to where a huge pile of slimy, twisted white roots were piled in a heap.

The greengrocer, bending down to put a match to the pyre, was knocked over and trampled by twenty webbed feet. By the time he finally managed to stand up again, Max, Hamfreda, the king, the queen, Horace, Caromel and Glom were all standing in a row, watching the geese happily gobbling Papparelli roots.

Scowling, he stamped his foot. "You're all mad! I want compensation! I'll be back tomorrow, and if I don't get my gold, I'll … I'll call every lawyer in the kingdom!" And he marched away, muttering.

The minute he was out of sight, Max's goose Violet laid an enormous golden egg. As the king and the queen gasped, she laid again … and then a third time. Looking extremely pleased with herself, she went to stand beside Max.

"Honk," she remarked. "Honk."

Chapter Seventeen

It wasn't until the following afternoon that another curious procession set out for the Wisest One's house. Caromel, who had gone home once the golden egg celebrations ended, had returned early the next day with an invitation for tea.

First in the procession was King Glom, driving the Glommet Six. King Ferdinand and Queen Gloria were perched on a tottering pile of cushions beside him: the queen looked nervous, but the king was enjoying himself enormously. He and Glom had spent the previous evening discussing the problems of kingship, and had agreed that a mutual trading arrangement would be most beneficial: a regular supply of gold in exchange for a regular supply of Papparelli roots. The geese, despite their hunger, had eaten only a fraction of the roots, and the remainder had been returned to the moat by the long-suffering greengrocer.

Max followed behind them riding Horace, whose owner had been much soothed by the promise of genuine gold, and had donated the donkey to the royal family in the hope of an even more substantial reward. Hamfreda and Caromel were keeping Max company, and the giant was also keeping a watchful eye on the Crimps, who were shut in the Glommet's trailer along with the fifteen remaining geese.

The would-be kidnappers were feeling very sorry for themselves. They had been allowed out of their bag, but the geese were uncomfortable companions; they trod all over the Crimps' feet and pecked them if they took up too much room.

When the cavalcade reached the Wisest One's house, Max wasn't entirely surprised to see the smoke message floating above the bent and crooked chimneys: *Welcome! Kindly progress to the garden. No vehicles allowed. Donkey may be included.*

"This way," Caromel said and she pranced forward to lead the way round the back of the house, through a tall arch and into a walled garden.

Roses covered the red brick walls, and poppies, lilies and delphiniums bloomed all around a square of bright green lawn where the Wisest One sat in an ancient basket chair. In front of her was a long table groaning under the weight of vast trays of sandwiches, deep bowls heaped high with biscuits, truly enormous cherry cakes, fruit cakes, chocolate cakes, lemon cakes and – towering above all else – a mighty iced edifice, with two flags flying at the top. Other chairs were arranged round the table, and Max was astonished to see that two were large enough to accommodate King Glom and Hamfreda.

"Sit yourselves down," the Wisest One ordered. "Caromel! Fetch the tea urn, if you please. And Maximilian, make yourself useful and bring the cups from the kitchen." She gave Hamfreda an assessing stare. "You can cut the cakes, young woman. You have a practical air about you."

Max, Hamfreda and Caromel did as they were told, and before long there was a contented silence as everyone ate and drank, then ate more and more. There was something about the Wisest One that encouraged silence; it was only after the plates were cleared away that King Ferdinand cleared his throat.

"I believe we must thank you, dear lady. Without help my son would never have achieved the triumph of restoring the fortunes of both my kingdom and the kingdom of my friend, King Glom." He stood up and bowed. "So I offer you my most sincere gratitude. And I'm sure that you would be interested to hear Maximilian tell you the story of his adventures, the success of which was entirely due to your most excellent advice—"

"Piffle." The Wisest One looked over her glasses at the king. "He did it because he's a sensible boy, although I can't think how he turned out so well when you took his books away."

She gave the king a chilly glance then looked at Max.

"Have you still got the book I gave you?"

Max nodded. "Oh, yes. Thank you." He pulled it out of his pocket. "Would you like it back?"

The Wisest One threw back her head and cackled with laughter.

"I gather you haven't looked at it today, boy. You'd be more enthusiastic if you had! Give it to me. I'll read it to you."

Max, wondering, did as he was told and the Wisest One took the book.

Then, giving her guests a commanding stare, she ordered, "Listen! Listen carefully and don't interrupt. This is a book I haven't yet read, and that is something to celebrate."

And she began to read.

"*In the kingdom of Little Slippington, things were not going well…*"

King Ferdinand sat bolt upright. "But that's MY kingdom—"

"Hush, dear," said Queen Gloria. "I do believe that this is Max's story." She settled herself more comfortably in her chair. "And I love having stories read to me, but—" a puzzled look came over her face— "I don't quite see how this one can be in a book already…"

"Never you mind about the hows." The Wisest One gave her an approving nod. "And you're quite right. This is the story of Maximilian's adventures. Now, as I was saying before I was so rudely interrupted:

Chapter One

In the kingdom of Little Slippington things were not going well.

"Does four and seven make forty?" King Ferdinand sounded hopeful...

(THE END!)

THE DRAGON'S
BREAKFAST

VIVIAN FRENCH

illustrated by Marta Kissi

THE DRAGON'S BREAKFAST

Princess Pom HATES being a princess! When a friendly
young orphan appears at the palace, she decides to run
away with him. She's after adventure and knows where
to find it: a treasure island. Legend has it there's pirate
gold, guarded by a fearsome dragon. Good thing Pom
isn't scared of dragons … or anything else!

THE **ADVENTURES** OF **ALFIE ONION**

THE **CHERRY PIE PRINCESS**

TOM & TALLULAH
AND THE
WITCHES' FEAST

Vivian French

lives in Edinburgh and writes in a messy workroom
stuffed full of fairy tales and folk tales – the stories she
loves best. She's brilliant at retelling classic tales, as she
did for *The Most Wonderful Thing in the World*, and has
created worlds of her own in *The Adventures of Alfie
Onion*, *The Cherry Pie Princess* and *Tom & Tallulah and
the Witches' Feast*. Vivian teaches at Edinburgh College of
Art and can be seen at festivals all over the country. She
is one of the most borrowed children's authors in UK
libraries, and in 2016 was awarded the MBE for services to
literature, literacy, illustration and the arts.

Marta Kissi

is a wonderfully talented illustrator, who came to Britain
from Warsaw to study Illustration and Animation at
Kingston University, then Art and Design at the Royal
College of Art. *The Dragon's Breakfast* is her fourth book
with Vivian French; her other work for children includes
books by Sophie Kinsella, Gillian Cross and Olympian Mo
arah. She shares a studio in London with her husband
d their pet plant Trevor.